Tom Lubben is a life-time educator, learner and dreamer. He resides in Northampton County with his wife Carole and has 26 extended family members scattered over six states. He has traveled extensively and uses this information in the creation of his books.

To Kay & Ron!
Enjoy the

Tom Lubben

To my wife, Carole, for her patience in dealing with me, and to my professional children who helped guide me.

Tom Lubben

Death Among the Pines

AUSTIN MACAULEY PUBLISHERS™

LONDON * CAMBRIDGE * NEW YORK * SHARJAH

Ordering Information
Quantity sales: Special discounts are available on quantity purchases by corporations, associations, and others. For details, contact the publisher at the address below.

Publisher's Cataloging-in-Publication data
Lubben, Tom
Death Among the Pines

ISBN 9781638291565 (Paperback)
ISBN 9781638291572 (Hardback)
ISBN 9781638291589 (ePub e-book)

Library of Congress Control Number: 2022901021

www.austinmacauley.com/us

First Published 2022
Austin Macauley Publishers LLC
40 Wall Street, 33rd Floor, Suite 3302
New York, NY 10005
USA

mail-usa@austinmacauley.com
+1 (646) 5125767

Table of Contents

Chapter 1
Vacation – August 1999

"Lord, Margaret, get those damned kids to sit down and be quiet!" An impatient father barked at his brood as he anxiously watched the creeping wand on his car thermostat. The air-conditioning light had winked off some thirty miles and two hours back on a one-lane highway between Philadelphia and Sea Isle City. The bright metallic paint on the '94 Chevy was designed for cooler climates and sucked in the day's heat like a metal vampire.

It was past noon and the late August sun hung ponderously over the scorched pine barrens of South Jersey. Water glistened over the marshland that they passed. His head pounded! Three kids bounced restlessly on the backseat among the debris of half-empty soda cans and assorted fast food wrappers...undistinguishable leftovers from an earlier lunch stop.

Summer pilgrims from a technologically paced world... Countless families have repeated the ritual of the trip to the Jersey shore over several modern generations. The cool ocean water and the hot sand drew folks from North Jersey via the New Jersey Turnpike, from Philadelphia over the Atlantic City Expressway and Canadians who streamed down the north to south highways. Anxious kids, overpacked cars, and overworked parents don't mix a smooth cocktail.

Yes, they come faithfully and ruthlessly, despite the risk of summer storms, jellyfish, and the occasional sharks. They contracted varied welts, fevers, and rashes from the myriad of diseases that still float down from the sewer outlets of Manhattan. Increasing numbers of dolphins, seals, and small whales seem to keep rolling in with the tides, bloated and dying from some underdetermined causes.

They come to bake. They come to cool. They thrive in the honky-tonk of Seaside and Wildwood; they luxuriate in the better bed and breakfasts in Cape

May and on rest on the quiet beaches of Long Beach Island. Young, intimate romances thrive with the boardwalk rituals. The middle-aged look to recapture that romance at nightclubs that cater to their youth, born here in the '50's and '60's. The aging population comes to the quiet spots to watch the surf do its magic to the shifting sands and to reflect on times past and prospects for whatever time they have left.

But the "Jersey Shore" began to shift and change as the casinos arrived in Atlantic City. Resorts International opened their doors to dramatic fanfare and publicity in 1978. Popular singer, Steve Lawrence, threw the first dice while Governor Brendan Byrne stood over his shoulder. (He lost $50.00 on the roll.) But generally, families didn't come for the casinos, but for the beaches and boardwalks. That's part of the reason that the nearby shore towns continued to thrive and grow. Kids could spend the day at the beach while and mom or dad could sneak down to the casino in the evening.

The family car moved slowly into another traffic jam as they entered a wider highway heading south. The surrounding pine-barrens were still scorched from a recent file. No smoke but the smell of charred wood still filters through the windows and air filtration system. Fires like that had become more common as careless smokers flicked their dying embers off into the woods. Behind them, thin trails of smoke still scroll like charcoal drawings across a clear canvas sky. You could still see some remnants of burnt out areas if you drove the length of the Pine Barrens.

As the car slowed, the restless kids focused on the road ahead. The line of cars stacked up to make way for the sirens and blinking lights of emergency vehicles. "Dead animal, Dad, dead animal ahead," shouted his son. They did much traveling and saw lots of road sites, but frequently a "dead animal" was just a "dead tire". They had experienced deer during the fall and winter in the Poconos, but usually not on this highway! But the jokes had a sense of pain as they drew closer to the scene.

Their attention shifted to a reddish, brown-black mass that most travelers generally swerved speed, or further desecrated the scene with an unfeeling tire. The remains of deer, stray dogs, skunk, or other varieties of small game are frequent sights that cars move swiftly past without much time to reflect or pity.

Who tends to these remains? What bizarre road crew rode the length of the state highways with buckets and shovels to remove the waste? Most road crews deal with the removal of newly killed deer; troopers are summoned to move the large dog; but most are left to the ravage of the evening wheels of big trucks, or the morning feast of carrion that hang patiently in the pines for just such food. Slowly, the poor dead thing that once "was", disintegrates into the totally undistinguishable glob of flood, flesh, and fur that marked this spot.

The family car moved slowly ahead in the Saturday shore traffic. The kids bounced excitedly, guessing the nature of the road "lump". The car came to an abrupt halt in response as a trooper stepped in front of their car to hold traffic while was allowing an emergency fire truck to come through for the pine barren fire.

The disgruntled father cursed again as an "idiot" light on his dashboard signaled a problem, and smoke became visible rising up from his hood. The car lurched to a stop close to the "dead animal" they had spotted. He went to pop the hood of the car, but first went around the car into the trunk for some cloths and gloves.

He almost tripped over the mass on the shoulder of the road. His curiosity got the best of him. He always had a fringe interest in the bizarre: either in a gruesome Steven King novel or a title on a supermarket tabloid. He pulled off his glasses to clear the fog that forms when you step out of an air-conditioned car into humidity.

A vague, unidentified stench penetrated his nostrils. He stumbled backward as his eyes began to focus on form of a lifeless mass. The brown, red, and black colors, combined with remnants of undistinguishable internal organs. A clearly visible severed hand lay in the midst of the horror. Blackened from fire, one finger was missing. This was a person! The fingers remaining held two perfectly sculpted black butterflies centered on the crimson nail.

The father bent over and promptly vomited the partially undigested remains of a Big Mac, fries, and a diet coke. He stood upright and bolted, mouth silently screaming, toward the trooper directing traffic!

State troopers approached the mess, as he stood frozen in place. "We'll take care of this, Sir, please return to your car." Honestly, however, the trooper had no idea what he was going to do with this mess!

The family watched as they pulled back on the road and continued their journey. They would not ever forget the horror of that moment, although they would let go of the terror to enjoy their next two weeks at the beach.

It was quite another matter for the troopers who were on the scene. This sight was considerably above their pay-grade. They rarely saw anything quite like this and they paused for a moment alongside of the body remnants. The trooper called in to his headquarters to report to his Captain who was equally concerned: "Don't touch anything until we send a forensic team out there!" The troopers covered the remains with plastic from the back of their car and waited, rather impatiently, for a team to come and get rid of this mess!

It would be an hour or so before a team from the local state police barracks would come and perform a rather rudimentary "cleanup", bagging the body parts and related debris, and taking it off to some undetermined destination.

Chapter 2
By the Sea – 27 December 1999

BJ was in the process of finishing his research concerning the early legends and stories of the natives in this area. He was planning on putting together a special unit on the history and tales of this region for his classes this coming fall. He had put his work away and took advantage of the clear air to walk the short distance to his view of the Atlantic Ocean.

Benjamin Jedidiah Gleeson was a solitary figure on that cold and empty beach. He stood several yards from the lapping surf that curled across smooth sand toward his sandals. He was 45 years old, the point in life where the term "mid-life crisis" creeps in. He had piercing brown eyes and his hairline was making its way back toward the middle of his head.

He looked at his watch; it was almost 10:30. The night sky was crisp and clear as he pulled his red windbreaker tighter over his lanky 6'1 frame. He did that for extra protection from the last winds of winter that blew crisply over the waves. On the horizon, two-night fishing boats traveled slowly across the line that separated the night sea from the night sky. Their small lights became a focal point for his vision. To the North, the lights of the tall casinos illuminated the coast of Atlantic City. To the South was darkness; summer rentals—deserted and emptied—were waiting for their July invasion. He stopped to pick up one of the large sconce shells that washed up on these empty beaches only during this time of the years.

It was two days after his loneliest Christmas ever. This would be his second Christmas alone. He and his ex-wife, Cassie, had parted ways over his wayward travels and sexually unwise experiences on that new device called the "Internet". The ink was not yet dry on their divorce agreement. His older son, James, had graduated from college, trained in the law, and relocated to Missouri; his daughter, Carly, just finishing her degree at Princeton!

The two kids were only separated by about three years. The young couple had argued a bit over their boy's name: However, BJ was a Bond fan and Cassie loved James Taylor. So James it was! When the girl arrived, BJ conceded to Cassie over Carly—as in Simon. Interestingly enough, that couple moved apart over the years.

The divorce was amicable, but lonely and painful just the same. Divorce, however, is never positive! He truly didn't keep in good enough contact with both children. There was a quiet hurt His daughter was fairly forgiving, but he had the most difficult time with his son! It was this personal torture that brought BJ to this part of the world—to escape. His ex-wife really wanted no part of him. She was rather successful now and focused her attention on their (now grown) children.

But BJ found a special mystical quality to these beaches, particularly at this time of the year. Without the crush of the vacationers, he enjoyed the solitude that this view offered. He was basically a loner and the pensive nature of the shore played into his melancholy. In that cold, crisp, air there existed a sense of eternal mystery as the sand and the sand continued to play out their relentless struggle with only the resilient gulls as their constant observers.

Lately, the sea had been winning. The New Jersey shore was steadily shrinking over the years, fall hurricanes along the coast washed out man made barriers and carried tons and tons of new sand backs to its bosom. During the day from now until Memorial Day you could watch trucks and large pipes pumping fresh white sand to replace the gains made by the sea.

BJ wondered about the generations who had walked these beached long before the condos, beach-houses, and board walks. His background as a part-time history teacher in north Jersey told him that there must have been endless stories that were made and told in these shifting sands. Each one washed back out to the memories that swirl in the ocean shores.

His imagination led him to wonder if any of his original Irish, German, or Jewish ancestors had contributed to this legacy, or had wandered to this special beach in their quest for life in this new world. He was half-Irish, and for sure, the Lynches and the O'Connors spent similar time on the rocks of the Irish Sea.

Somehow, through the sound of the surf and the wind, BJ finds a quietness here that is unmatched. God never seemed more real than when he comes here. His thoughts seemed to crystalize with the bright stars that never are so bright.

He would capture poetry out of this night—if anyone wanted to read them! His sad poetry collection remained in an old yellow folder in one of the desk drawers in his new apartment. He often thought about a career as a writer based on this area, but the reality of a life and a job got in the way of that dream.

The tall, lanky figure turned and began walking toward the far off lights of Atlantic City. He stooped occasionally to pick up an odd shell, aimlessly kicking at a spare piece of driftwood. Every so often, a couple stroll slowly but on the boardwalk, but basically, he is alone—with his thoughts, his dreams, and his problems. He has always marked milestone in his life at these special places.

He came here, alone, to mark the passing (separately) of both his mother and father. They were the ones who had first showed him the shoreline. He was an only child born to older parents. He had been indulged with time at the Jersey Shore throughout his youth. Mom and Dad scraped together funds for one week every year. His father's old '36 Desoto needed two gallons of water every twenty miles to survive the trip. They frequently returned to their North Jersey apartment with only a few coins on their person. This was before the ATM and people didn't cash Northerner's checks in Seaside!

He went to a state college, not on his grades, but on a baseball scholarship. He struggled through the course-work until he met his first love, Cassie, who was much brighter than him. Cassie carried him through his academic struggles, while he concentrated on Baseball. They married straight out of college and he signed a small minor league baseball contract.

She would stake out an apartment in Hackensack, while he traveled for five months of the year. Not an ideal relationship setting. He managed to get her pregnant a few times on his trips home and his winter. He had acquired a teaching degree so that he could substitute during the winter when the season was over.

BJ found nothing but loneliness on his minor league journey. The "only child syndrome" followed him like a curse. He was truly a loner. He found himself escaping from the party atmosphere on the road. He was basically a one-woman man and couldn't bring himself to indulge in the loose activities of his teammates.

His parents hadn't raised him in the church, although his mother had been a Catholic and his dad a Lutheran. They compromised when they got married and stopped going to church at all. His mother, however, did teach him the bedtime prayers and Christmas carols. As a young teen, a neighbor persuaded him to attend a non-denominational church where he had his first (of many) direct confrontations with Jesus Christ.

His wife, Cassie, brought him to a more formal church and he personally devoted many quiet moments to a reflection about his faith, his life, and his future. He had developed a powerful belief in God and the Holy Trinity, but still struggled with the faith that would allow him to put himself in God's hands and not go it alone. Every night as he recited the Lord's Prayer, he amended, "Thy will be done…" with the added words, "Not mine!"

During that journey, when his teammates headed for the local whorehouses or pickup joints, he stayed back in his hotel room and swallowed himself up in his reading. He particularly enjoyed reading about local history. When they were on the road, he would look up the stories that existed about the towns they were traveling through. He was creating a life in his head with his readings. At the same time, he was avoiding coming to grips with his lack of positive relationships.

Some thirty years later, here he is back on the solitary beaches of South Jersey, trying to put his life back together.

He started making the long trips to this quiet beach when his fastball lost its hop and his curve ball could no longer get passed strong young minor leaguers. They passed him up on their way to the show. He had to decide, then, what a washed up ballplayer at age thirty-two could do with the rest of his life.

Ex-minor leagues don't do commercials for ABC or serve as commentators on ESPN. (Even though he twirled a no-hitter in the D League and led the league in strikeouts while playing for San Antonio in the Triple-A leagues— one step from the top!) So he moved from the "diamond" to, eventually, the full-time classroom!

But BJ understood that the bulk of the blame for his relationship failures had been of his own doing. He was guilty, not only of the Internet excursions, but he was, also, a lost soul with respect to his career and to his future. He still was in the midst of that struggle. Sure, he had just landed a job as a full time teacher and a coach. But was that to satisfy his inquisitive nature? But for now, that nature didn't give him any direction or help with his relationships.

For now he thought the Jersey Shore would be the focal point of a great career and the rest of his life. But deep down, he was searching for something else. Would he find it here? Or would he forever muddle through life? When he got back to his apartment, he would spend the rest of the evening reading about the Native Americans who originally inhabited this area from an old journal he had obtained from the local historical society.

He looked at his watch again—past 11:30 already! He kicked the sand off his sandals as he climbed back up to the boardwalk and walked down the empty street to his waiting dark red Nissan mini-van. He would head back to his apartment, put away his equipment, run a fast razor over his face and go visit a new friend he had made in one of the shore joints that would still be open. But first, he wanted to revisit the Native American piece he had just uncovered.

Chapter 3
Late Spring – 1630

BJ began his reading:

Shingas struggled as he pulled his heavily laden wood canoe onto the shore. His wife, A'Shatama, helped guide and steadied their valuable load. Their trip to the sea had been bountiful and been blessed by all the gods to whom they gave service and reverence. Several times each year they made this long trip to the sea together. Their small inland Absegame tribe treasured their catch.

Much of the sea bass and eels were eaten in a homecoming celebration while the remained was salted and cured for sustenance between trips and over the cold winter. Venison, bear, and wolves and raccoon were standard fare. The sea catch provided a natural balance that their innate bodies craved and loved.

They had traveled for two days close to what is today, the Tuckahoe River, leading into the mouth of Great Egg Harbor that leads into the sea between Ocean City and Atlantic City. At the vast harbor they encountered members of other small tribes that famed and fished in the nearby areas. They were friendly, and basically agrarian, unlike the projections of European literature that had historically painted them as warlike barbarians in order to justify their systematic removal and elimination.

They often spent several days trading tales and sharing history with these old friends who welcomed their period visits. Increasingly, they heard tales of strange men with broad-brimmed hats and pale faces that sailed into these harbors with huge boats, hoisting large pieces of canvas that seemed to stretch endlessly into the cloudless blue skies over the water.

Initially cruel and barbaric, the visitors used a long spear that spit fire and hurled hot-small arrows that tore deep into the flesh of the natives. Too many had already tasted death from those 'fire sticks'. For others, however, the friendly natives established a positive pattern for trade and exchange.

But these strangers were more of a myth to the simple people like Shingas and A'Shatama. They lived their lives in relative isolation from the rest of the rapidly changing world. Their relationships were very family and tribal focused. Yes, there were other tribes, and some of them seemed quite strange. But they lived in reasonably isolation within their own tribe. Comfortable and oblivious to the world outside their small region. Shingas had not yet met any of these strange new people, although he heard similar tales from the people North of the Delaware, who had indicated that these visitors were beginning to make their presence felt in many places around them.

Shingas and A'Shatama used simples nets take their catch. Small sticks were shaped and used to float the nets. The figure of the stick resembled their one of their devil gods—Manitto. The "stick gods" would begin to shake and twist at the fish would enter the net. The couple would sing out in praise to the great Manitto for giving them a good catch. Their "faith" was rather simple and related directly to the elements that greatly controlled their lives. Like the Romans of ages past, they developed God's to reflect varied aspects of their lives: food, love, children, work, and the other aspects of a simple life.

The canoe drifted noiselessly toward home; A'Shatama remarked to Shingas, "How marvelous that we can return to our beautiful village settled so deep in the Pines. There we can raise our sons and daughters in peace and comfort in honor of our gods." They had packed their canoe carefully for the long trip back upstream. Larger fish had been stripped and cleaned to reduce the travel weight. Only a few of the succulent shell fish could be carried all the way home, so the couple spent most of their last night at sea with a feast of fresh clams, shrimp, and crab.

Now with their canoe safely tucked in the thicket, for a return next Spring, A'Shatama prepared a makeshift bed of dried pine needles while Shingas prepared a fire for them to cook and warm themselves in this cool October evening. Lacking books, television, cell-phones, and written language, the history of memories of the Absegame were shared by stories spoken over and over again at the evening fires, or during the long trips through the endless Pine Barrens.

Tonight, Shingas was reminded of an old legend that became more important as the stories of the white invaders increased in fear and foreboding.

For the elders of long ago had passed down a strange tale of an olive-skinned visitor with long, tightly curled hair, and an odd tongue. He arrived in the midst of the Pines further back in time then any could imagine. He came to live among the Absegame. He became one of them and began to share a strange message of love and peace that frightened and threatened some of the young men of the tribe.

Legend had it that he had begun to surround himself with a small group of tribesmen, and stories began to emerge about strange miracles and healings. The small band began to see vision when in the company of this man.

After about a year, some elders, fueled with the fear of other younger men, had called for this stranger's execution. Seized one night, he was bludgeoned unconscious and tied to two large pieces of wood shaped in a large X. He was then burned alive, his ashes and bones consigned to rocks in a shallow grave. Some claimed that this grave had vanished but many claimed to have seen a longhaired, olive-skinned figure wandering through the Pines or traveling the inland waters in a small canoe.

Here and there, tales of additional healings and miracles in his presence were described. The elders and leaders had pledged his death to the potent god of darkness that shadowed much of their religion.

Manito's strength and dominance was threatened by the prospect of a return from this odd stranger. Over the many years there were continued times and seasons of such similar sacrifices and executions. Abruptly, A'Shatama stopped Shingas in his tale of these strange tales, in an attempt to quietly return their thoughts to their return trip.

In one day, they would be back to their two young sons. The sons who now spent time picking the wild berries with the older women of the tripe. The same sons who would soon begin to move out to hunt and fish with the strong men and women of the tribe. These sons, who would, in several years, select their mate from the beautiful young girls who spent time learning the skills of their mothers.

Water was so important to the Absegame. It was plentiful in the clear inland streams and lakes; more powerful in the rivers that pounded toward the bay. At the head of the bay, where the Ocean met; tumultuous waves crashed over rocks, destroyed small craft, and sucked away those that walked those primal shores. Their sons had been exposed to a longstanding tradition with the water.

Shortly after A'Shatama gave birth, Shingas carried the newborn to the nearest cold, rushing stream and quickly plunged the screaming infant under the water. Many infants died through this brutal exposure to the elements, but survival guaranteed strength and courage to the baby who would become the young brave. Their two sons had both survived this tradition. One other child had ceased breathing and died within two days of the ceremony.

A'Shatama talked quietly and musically about her boys, her hopes, and their dreams as the fire burned warm and bright. They wrapped themselves in a warm blanket. Shingas began to talk about his fears of this new people, but A'Shatama put a finger to his lip to quiet him. Her other hand moved softly down his chest to his loins. He murmured softly as he felt his soul tingle and his body stiffen. His hands returned the gentle stroking and they made love repeatedly until—when totally exhausted—they fell asleep clinging tightly to one another.

At daybreak they rose together, washed in the river, and collected their catch for the overland walk that would bring them to their village by evening. Fully loaded, they began their walk along a long but familiar trail through the pines. These trails had been used for generations. Narrow paths curved endlessly through the tall majestic trees. They moved down the familiar paths lacking the street signs or GPS of today.

The vastness of the pine-barrens shifted between opulent beauty and rough-hewn areas that had been scarred by fire or overgrown by ugly vines that carried thorns—but no fruit that anyone would care to eat. Their trip brought the Absegame family though all of this. The cranberry bogs had a late fall tinge of red that carried over acres of marshland. The growth of the pine trees provided a rich background in all shades of red and green.

The paths were limited to single file and Shingas led the laden-down procession of two on a study, uninterrupted pace toward home. They had eaten before they left and would not stop until they reached their village. Suddenly, off to his left, Shingas saw the distant wisps of smoke that indicated the beginning of a "burning". The common practice for hunting deer, then, was to establish backfires in the perimeter of an area with about a one-mile perimeter.

Loud noises would drive the deer to the center of a small circle where the tribe could easily kill many with their bows and spears. Early Europeans often reported this burning. They often described South Jersey by the "sweet perfume" that filled the air for miles: the result of the burning pine trees.

Silently, the couple moved on westward. Conversation would sap the strength that they needed on this, the final leg, of this final march. They moved closer to the spires of smoke and tired noticeably as the sun rose to noonday. Suddenly, Shingas realized that his path was taking him directly into the firs. The smell of fresh burnt pine entered his nostrils with a strange, undefinable fear. One could not leave the established path without being totally lost in the vast pines, so Shingas had to press head to quickly get to a fork in the path that would move him away from the fires.

He picked up the pace to a slow trot, dragging his load. A'Shatama, sensing his fear and knowing his strategy, tried to pick up her pace, but fell further behind them as they moved toward the smoke and fire. She was losing him. Their breaths were coming in long gasps, Shingas' muscles began to throb and cramp. Sweat ran down his face and chest. He could not drop his load, and hopefully, the fork would be there soon. They might have to take a detour, but they would be safe in each other's arm again that evening.

He looked back over his shoulder but could not see her through the winding turns of the route. He was not immediately worried since she often fell behind him, particularly toward the end of their journey.

He believed he could feel the heat of the encroaching fire as he finally saw the fork that would relieve their pace not far ahead. By know he could see flames locking over the tops of trees off to his right. As he got nearer to the fork, he felt the growing force of the fire and smoke, the air was far hotter than what the noonday sun would provide. He looked behind, and began to worry— A'Shatama was nowhere in his view and he was quickly approaching the source of the fire.

As he turned onto the new path, Shingas was confronted with a sight that challenged his senses and shot fear through every nerve in his body. Several hundred yards ahead stood a burning tree in the center of the path. Through a smoky fog, he saw that the tree was engulfed in a raging fire that seemed separate from the burning they had been escaping. As he moved closer to the tree, his senses perceived several images simultaneously. A strong smell permeated his nostrils, not quite the odor of roasting venison.

Strange low, guttural, and painful sounds emerged from the charred mass lased to the tree. At the same time, a huge man, wearing a brightly colored mask, stepped out in front of him. Shingas' eyes were drawn to the strange markings that covered his unclothed body, vaguely reminding him of religious symbols. Vivid-colored crosses seemed to be imprinted on his dark-skinned body.

The man stopped his chanting and turned toward Shingas with a foreboding stare. He turned and pointed to the figure lashed to the tree and laughed hideously. In this, his final moment of life, Shingas recognized in terror that it was the body of A'Shatama that was lashed to that tree. The upraised hand of the smiling killer was holding her bloody, severed hand skyward. This was his last vision on earth, as a blunt object from behind crushed his skull and silenced his memories for ever…

BJ Gleeson quietly laid down his book, *The Early History of the Jersey Pines* in front of him and decided he had read enough for this evening! As his trips took him through much of the area, he often reflected on what life might have been in the near and far past. He was fascinated with the long rich history of this mysterious territory and was dedicated to learning more about the past in this region.

Chapter 4
Staley's Tavern

BJ put down the journal and slipped his notes into a yellow file folder.

BJ had found a seldom-used, small, one-bedroom, furnished apartment in Sea Isle City. It had been established as a vacation rental, but it was on the less inviting bayside of the City—still two blocks away from (even) bay water. The owners were glad to have a year-round tenant for what would have been a hard-to-rent space. He had a fairly new TV in a small living room with a pull-out couch in case he ever had guests. It was perfect for his new situation.

Shore towns are known for their bars! But most remain closed and vacant from October through May. Here and there, however, a place like Staley's, survive because the locals need some place to go year round. Staley's wasn't a typical beach-bar. It sat rather obscurely back from the road, just off a major junction on Route 9. A small poorly lit sign and a parking lot semi-full of cars were indications that life was still there!

The inside provided a stark contrast to the bland offerings from the road. It was almost 12:30 before Gleeson took his seat at the end of the bar and perused the Friday night crowd. Most lighting was provided by the collection of old beer advertisements scattered around the large circular bar.

The Anheiser-Busch stallions chased each other endlessly around the huge globe light that hang in the center of the room. A few televisions scattered around the walls carried a combination of sporting events and the late night cooking shows. Two pool tables sat, lonely tonight, in the corner of the room. Old stuffed booths, attached to the walls, were scattered around the perimeter. In the far corner stood an empty bandstand, waiting for the arrival of the summer crowd.

Magic marker menus hung on the walls, indicating special cheap fare that kept the place busy throughout the year. Prices went up for the "shoe-bees" who came every summer. BJ didn't even know what "shoe-bees" were until he spent time in South Jersey. Seems that the people who came down from the North—just for the day—packed their stuff in a shoe box which they left on the beach while they rollicked in the waves.

The Southerners—some of them pure "Pineys"—still were not completely comfortable with the northern intruders. This became worse after gambling came to Atlantic City. Housing prices in the region soared as "newbies" relocated from the North once they acquired jobs in Atlantic City. This frustrated young Southerners who saw their potential for buying a cheap home evaporate with the onslaught from the North-Jersey folks. There was no love lost between the two groups. Builders were cashing in on purchasing cheap parcels of land and constructing three and four bedroom "mac-mansions" that sold for twice the cost of similar existing homes.

At Staley's, for now, the local farmers, fisherman, realtors, construction workers, and Atlantic City Employees would indulge in the benefit of a five-dollar steak and cheese and a $3 small pitcher of Coors light! This was a typical South Jersey crowd at this point in the year.

The bar crowd was thinning out, with only the regulars left to hold down the conversation—and to keep the three bartenders company until closing. A few couples were scattered around, but the leftovers at the bar were all men. Staley's wasn't a "meat-market"—except for the summer when the husbands left their bored wives down for the entire summer.

While their men went back to their work and/or affairs, these temporarily single women became the summer mainstays at the bar during the week, until their husbands got down for the weekend. They were safe alternatives to the hookers who frequented some of the nearby Atlantic City locations. And cheaper too!

Gleeson had only lived in this area for a little over a year, but he was already an established veteran at Staley's. He discovered this place by accident one evening. He had just taken a teaching job at Central Pineland Regional High School (Pinelands Regional, as the locals called it…)—a "rookie" again, this time at almost 50 and not on a baseball diamond. The regulars were beginning to accept him despite his Northern roots.

After his divorce, he had packed up, left his substitute teaching positions that he held in several Northern Counties, to accept the job of teacher in the Social Studies Department and as head baseball coach. The school was a relatively new, sprawling complex, located almost 20 miles inland—in the heart of the Pine Barrens.

He had connected with an old friend from North Jersey, Clarke Matthews, who had been a Principal in Jersey City. Now he had a fresh start. Central hadn't had a winning season since their inception, and BJ's 1-21 start did not bode well for his future! Good players were scarce. By springtime, the stronger athletes from football and basketball were heading out for relatively lucrative part-time jobs. Construction at Atlantic City continued to heat up. Renovations on shore homes were another good place for some work. He was stuck recruiting from lesser athletes.

He sucked down an Absolut Seabreeze that the bartender had automatically placed in front of him and swiveled his stool to look around the room. The typical crowd was a mix of business suits and long-bearded country folk: It was truly Wall Street meets Duck Dynasty!

As his eyes continued to scan the room, he saw her swing out through the kitchen doors. Newcomers to Staley's often mistook Jade Staley-Brinkman as a descendant of one of the Indian tribes that initially inhabited the region— generations earlier. Her deeply tanned skin in combination with long, brown, straight hair that fell to her waist—contributed to that image. Tall, slim with long legs and firm small breasts, she looked like a carefree girl only a few years out of college. Her long feathered earrings further contributed to her mystique. She didn't look like a life-scarred, tough, 39-year-old part owner of a successful shore restaurant.

The restaurant had been one of several in the state that her Father, Rudolph Staley had carefully nurtured based on a combination of location and cliental potential. After the death of her parents, Jade had inherited a part-ownership in this location. Ten years earlier, she had taken her (then) six-year old daughter, Justine, down to the Cape May Area to face the challenges of a single-mom in a tough shore bar with a new home in the middle of the Pines!

BJ knew she was no Indian. They had grown up only miles apart in Northern New Jersey. They attended the same schools, but at different times. They never knew each other until they met, by accident, in a North Jersey church. He was separated from his wife, she—recently divorced—from her first husband.

He caught her eye and, at the end of the service, asked her, "How was your Christmas?"

"Shitty," she replied.

BJ simply said "me too" and they exchanged telephone numbers. Several months passed before he got the courage to call her. He was not yet divorced but they began to find reasons to get together. They then began to meet to commiserate on their problems—both in North Jersey and subsequently in her new home in South Jersey.

He had first walked into the bar some months earlier—quite by accident. They had lost touch with each other as they both moved through their relationship problems. He was excited at the prospect of truly getting to really know her. Her charm and upbeat style brought a smile to his somber mood on those early bad nights in South Jersey. As they shared their pasts, they were both surprised to find their common roots and a warm bond quickly developed.

Gleeson had not completely separated (mentally) from his first love and wife and Jade sensed that! Although they had moved far away, the shambles of his life still left him with a raw heart. Long absences due to his baseball journey didn't help them at all. He had staggered in and out of partial relationships over the past few years—and throughout his hapless minor-league experience. He was more than grateful that he had finally met someone who could somewhat identify with his past.

His wife never knew of her, but there were several close calls. He foolishly decided to bring his two kids to surreptitiously meet her. Fortunately, weather intervened! On another day, he almost had tickets for both his wife and Jade at a conference in the Meadowlands—in different parts of the arena. He was desperately working on a plan that involved taking each one separately, then forging an excuse to get the second one into her seat—and bounce between the two locations in the arena.

Neil Diamond was a hot ticket! This had all the makings of a sitcom gone bad, but Jade couldn't get away from her family—so BJ was saved again. BJ might have been a reasonably bright individual—but his relationship skills were sorely lacking.

It was over a year since their first meetings, and the bond was developing into a complex relationship that both troubled and soothed them both. BJ was finally divorced, but could they be friends AND lovers? For now, however, they enjoyed their stalemated situation. Both were still so deeply involved in their "prior" families and careers that this had to suffice for the present. She moved down to his seat on the bar, leaned over, and gave him a gentle kiss on his cheek: "Let's get a table over in the corner, the kitchen's still open and I need to get something to eat."

She ordered two more drinks and they sat together in a small booth, where they unloaded the problems of their respective week. BJ shared his frustration with unskilled ballplayers, uninterested students, and a still troubled family in the North and elsewhere! Jade spoke of keeping the help out of the cash registers and trying to rope in a restless 16-year-old daughter. She also ranted about her ex-husband who tried to avoid paying his part of her daughter's life as much as he could.

Waitresses were now long gone. One of the kitchen help brought out a large plate of nachos with hot cheese, refried beans, and crisp green jalapenos. Gleeson had a penchant for hot foods, playing a lot of ball in the Texas league. Jade smiled as his eyes teared from the flaming peppers.

The bartenders were beginning to clean up and tally for the evening. Jade, as part owner, needed to be there until the doors were locked. This was not an easy gig for a single mom! BJ wondered how she could manage all of this along with a home in the Pines, three dogs, and a teen-age daughter.

A solitary figure staggered in through the front door. BJ had never seen the woman before, but Jade recognized her immediately and welcomed her: "Annie, what brings you here at this late hour?"

"My daughter, my daughter," she croaked despondently. She moved, drunkenly, toward a nearby table and slumped into the chair. "How 'bout one before closing, Stan?" She groped into her large purse for some money.

"Looks like you've had enough for tonight, kid," said Stan as he looked questioningly toward Jade and BJ.

"Give her just one scotch, on the house, Stan," said Jade, in sympathy.

Chapter 5
Pine-Bog Annie

Whores were uncommon at Staley's and most of the shore bars. There was plenty of free action to make a prostitute's decent income a real disability. The men didn't really need to drive North to Atlantic City with the plethora of well-tanned shore moms who frequented Staley's as well as so many other places. Annie fit the stereotype of the 42nd St. hookers of old, but had the carriage of a bag lady. Neither was typical of South Jersey. Overly made up, with a faded blouse stretched tight over her melon-shaped breasts: she looked hard and old! Gleeson guessed she was over 60 and was shocked when Jade later told him that she was in her late 40s.

Although a stereotype for NYC, Annie was too typical of a breed of prostitutes who plied their trade along Route 9 for generations. Route 9 existed a long time before the Garden State Parkway was even under consideration. It was THE route to the shore. You drove over the Pulaski Skyway in Newark and caught Route 9 just over the river. Even after the advent of the Parkway, many truckers (avoiding the tolls) took the "old" route to many their South Jersey stops. Kerosene lanterns along the roadside became familiar landmarks to identify the hookers.

Annie had developed a reputation as "Pine-Bog Annie" among the truckers. Her lantern was posted on a slope of the road near a Cranberry Bog. At a nearby rest stop, she would meet them in their spacious cabs…dousing her light until her services had been completed.

Life changed for Annie and the other whores once gambling was approved. The nature of the trade dramatically changed. As a near 40-year-old, Annie was being passed by with the fast life that had hit the boardwalk in AC. The more successful whores nixed the highway trade for Atlantic City. They watched the papers and flocked to AC for plumber and fireman conventions, but avoided the teacher's convention like the plague ("bunch of cheap-skates" was the word…).

The "trade" passed Pine-Bog Annie by! At plus 40, she no longer had the ability to draw clients. Further, alcohol and drugs began reaching into her earlier beauty. She lost her stamina and was left as a tired-shell of a woman. Annie stopped here occasionally, not to ply her trade, but for a nightcap before she headed back into the pines to her ram-shackled cabin. Jade had watched her disintegrate over the ten years she had been at Staley's and truly pitied her existence.

She became a sad fixture at Staley's. She was largely left alone, milking a drink at the end of the bar or at a corner table. Always alone; Jade felt sorry for her. She tried her best to befriend the poor woman whenever she had a chance. Annie would occasionally share sad stories about her upbringing in the Pine Barrens and, on her rare "up days"; try to regale Jade with her early glory days, plying the trade in Atlantic City. Her entrance always panged at the heart of the sensitive Jade.

Annie drained her scotch quickly and laid her head down on the table. She began to moan, tears stained her make-up caked cheek and ran in rivulets down to the tablecloth. Jade left their booth and moved quickly across the room to comfort her.

BJ, out of curiosity, walked slowly toward Annie's table. It was none of his business, but he had seldom seen Annie and he was drawn to her by her obvious sorrow. He was also impressed with the tenderness that Jade demonstrated to the woman. He was not always regarded as the most sensitive man, but something powerful drew him into their portion of the room.

"My daughter, my daughter, Princess Kelly, where are you?" Annie sobbed.

Jade offered: "What can we do to help, where is Kelly?"

Annie wiped at her eyes with the end of the tablecloth. Tears and make-up came off together. She spoke, haltingly, through her tears… "Kelly ran away, at least I thought she did, this past summer. We always fought. I didn't want her in this trade—but she had to have her own way. I thought she would come back—but not like this!" She coughed to clear her throat and reached down into her large purse. Jade's arm was around Annie's shoulder. BJ stood over them in concern.

Annie brought out a small ceramic box, hand-painted with flowers of a red and purple shade. It resembled a miniature jewelry box. She slowly opened the box and peeled back that velvet cloth that held the "treasure". Jade's hand dropped to the table. BJ started at the sight.

In a bizarre flashback, Gleeson was reminded of a sophomoric prank that kids frequently pulled: Take a small box, put some ketchup and a hole on the bottom. Then put your finger through the hole. Really spooked the girls! Looked just like a severed finger. But, no joke this time!

In that same instance, he realized, too clearly, that the ceramic box did indeed contain a severed finger that was not the produce of a joke! Sitting against the backdrop of black velvet sat a finger that was beginning to shrivel and dry, a finger no longer with blood. The fingernail was clearly polished a distinctly sculpted butterfly delicately and professional added to the center. "That's my Kelly's finger," Annie exclaimed as she passed out cold in Jade's arm.

BJ carried the light body of the despondent woman back into Jade's office and stretched her out on the old couch nestled in the corner of the room. Jade walked in behind him with a pot of coffee and a wet rag. Annie was quickly revived, and quickly sucked down the coffee that was to help her regain her sobriety and (hopefully) her sanity.

Jade and BJ talked quietly while she gained some composure. The image of the finger was a shock to both of them. But, what could they do with this? How could they help? This woman had no one else to turn to and they had to provide her with some support and guidance.

BJ, the amateur historian, was thinking about the nature of that small box and the unique design on her daughter's finger. This seemed to tweak a memory from his many historical readings about this part of the state. But what was it? He had lots of notes in his small apartment that he could review when he got back to Sea Isle. But for now, they both had to give their full attention to Annie.

Slowly and laboriously, Pine-Bog Annie began to tell her own story.

But even before she began speaking, BJ's "history" of this area began to flow back into his primary consciousness. Now, the Pine Barrens are crisscrossed with the NJ Parkway, Turnpike (further north) and countless newer wide roads and side roads that seem to go to nowhere. But more than one million miles of pines offered people a very cheap place to live.

Route 9 runs down along the Jersey Coast straight Cape May. Running East-West are roads like the Blackhorse Pike and Whitehorse Pike. These roads run parallel to one another. These roads pre-date revolutionary times and have always led people to the sea. Once populated by horse-drawn carriages and slow-moving motorcars, improved paving and dramatic widening have provided a fast lane to the sea. Many smaller roads intersect with these main thoroughfares and often lead lost travelers or inquisitive investigators into the heart and soul of the Pine Barrens.

A "right turn" for a traveler on the "wrong" way to Atlantic City can take him into some uncharted paths through the pines! At one of his earliest visits to the area, BJ was leaving a woman's home late in the evening, got lost in the barrens until he finally found a brand new-highway, with no cars, that eventually got him back to North Jersey by 3:00 AM. For a reasonably small state, the Pine Barrens could be rather foreboding for untrained travelers.

Here the curious of mind can discover the "Pineys": People known through the history and eastern mythology as the hillbillies of the East. There are occasional stories about people in this region with a sixth finger on one hand: probably a product of close inter-breeding! Annie's roots were here! Her soul had been shaped by those tall pines—so close to megalopolis and yet to remote from today.

The presence of Lenape Indians, escaped slaves, and deserted British soldiers (from Scotland and Ireland) began to mix and intermingle in the protection and solitude that the Pines afforded to people who had nowhere else to hide. Even the fabled legends of the "Jersey Devil" stemmed back to a Piney Woman, Mother Leeds, who was said to have given birth to her 13th child that emerged half-human and half-devil. The creature flew off into the skies! Legend says this was in 1735.

But Annie was born of no great mystery. Her parents were true Pineys, with no great historical legacy and no sixth finger! No claims to the throne of England, nor Tribal chieftains. They were simple migrant workers in the Vineland area. Annie's parents came to the Pines on a great deal. In the 1920s, a Philadelphia newspaper was offering free lots for a subscription. The purchase price for a lot in the Pines was $5.00! Many other people took advantage of the open land and property.

They were hard workers who traveled east to Atlantic City to obtain winter work as domestics in the emerging hotel (pre-casino) trade.

Born in 1950 in a simple three-room wood-frame house in the central pines; Annie quickly became the classic immigrant worker child. She rarely trekked out to the area schools, and the schools were not particularly interested in "hunting" for absent or truant students in the pines. At 16, Annie believed she had found her profession. She was presently picking cranberries and peeling soiled sheets off vacation beds. Life had to offer more.

She would slip out of their rented AC house to witness the "Jewels of the Boardwalk". Brightly adorned and mod-as-mod could be in 1968, these ladies of the evening sparked like jewels in Annie's restless young eyes. Her shape had just begun to round into the natural curves of womanhood and her large breasts, coupled with a small waist made her a willing target.

A black pimp broker her in—painfully—left her twenty dollars and placed her with one of the girls in his stable. The shame and pain overcame that initial glamour, and Annie bolted from the other woman and fled back to her family before he had time to press her into active service. Her parents couldn't contend with the quiet morose youth who wouldn't leave her bed, go to school, or even go to work with them. They shrugged dejectedly, weeping quietly over their poor fate as they went back to their lives in the fields.

Some months later, Annie broke out of her melancholy and the shame of her existence. She found her $20 award that she had hidden among her things. She packed what little she had and left! She ended up at an old diner that was at the intersection of the Whitehouse pike and the dirt road that led back towards her old home.

She was quickly adopted by a small group of women who worked the Truckers out of Atlantic City. They hung out in the diner in the late morning, drinking black coffee and choking on long cigarettes while they shared funny anecdotes and their dreams.

"Stay out of AC, baby," said one young woman in her late twenties. "Pimps don't want no part of the Piney trade. Truckers are straight fuckers and occasional blowjobs with no percentage for some boss-man," she sneered. "Find a good spot on the highway where you can stand and attract attention." Annie improved on that by hanging out a lantern that became her personal symbol.

"Pick your times for heading to AC," said another. "Good conventions with big bucks (and little pricks)"—the others all laughed. "And go solo, so you can bring all of those dollars back here to rest in the Pines."

And Pine-Bog Annie (as she came to be known) did just that. Her young, healthy form quickly became known among the long-haul truckers who shared their good news on their CBs. Annie had found a small rise along the road, about 300 yards from a quiet rest stop and picnic area. When her glowing lantern hung on one sparse tree, truckers knew that "Pine-Bog Annie" was open for business!

When a willing truck pulled in, Annie would cover her light—if the trucker flashed his light three times, Annie would climb down the hill and walk slowly to the cab. Annie's actions depended on the man's rig, the time available to both parties, or the interest the young woman had in listening to the tales of travel from these mysterious, seasoned road-warriors.

Sometimes, she would clamber up into the cab that often resembled a small motel room, perform her services, and quickly clean up and clamber back down the full-sized rig. Often, she would lead a customer back into an area she had cleared under a grove of tall pine trees. The ground was soft with the covering of years of pine needed, and she had managed to hide a small, old wooden trunk that contained a sizeable blanket and a few cheap thro-pillows.

Some men liked to be listened to almost as much as they liked to make love and Annie quickly learned to become a good listener for them. She learned far more about the life and world around her in that clearing then she ever had in the sterile classrooms she had so seldom visited.

Her rude introduction to sex had savagely hardened her against warm intimacy. Only occasionally did a customer begin to break through her protective shell that had enabled her to survive in this bizarre trade. Big Mac was such a man. There weren't any McDonald's in the Pines, yet. But she quickly developed to this man who drove a huge red truck with the emblems of the company emblazoned along the sides.

Annie began to see Big Mac almost once a week. He was an independent trucker who stopped at her lantern coming back from Newark and heading to exotic points South. Mac was around 40 years old, about 6'4, with a full head of curly silver hair. Annie quickly noticed that his rig was decorated with the picture of three kids and a rather homely woman, who she figured was his wife.

Annie had been plying her trade, now, for about 15 years or so. She never allowed herself get "caught", used protection, insisted on the men using condoms... No kids for Annie. And (until Big Mac) no love either. But he soon got the best of her… She saw qualities in him that she never saw in her other Johns.

Initially, they would engage in quick, rough, passionate (for him) sex. He'd then open up a bottle of wine and they would lie in the soft pines while he spoke of the Florida Everglades, the Tobacco Farms of the South, and the bright lights of Washington, DC. Annie began to think she could now "feel" while she was with Mac.

Their lovemaking became less rough and more sensitive. In the deep recesses of her mind, she subconsciously began to think of love. But as quickly as Mac had appeared—he was gone! Several weeks after, Annie noticed that her period was late. Although Big Mac wasn't her only trucker, it pleased her to believe that this seed growing inside her was his seed.

She continued to ply her trade, hoping to see Big Mac again, until she realized that the sight of a very pregnant 32-year-old was not very appealing to a trucker. It was 1982 and she spent her remaining "time" hanging out with the other girls during the day, smoking two packs a day, drinking black coffee, and talking the time away.

One week after her own birthday, she gave birth to (what would be) her only child. She was a kicking, screaming baby with the biggest steel-grey eyes she had ever seen. Annie's mom served as a mid-wife and with the exception of a few visits to a local clinic, the two women brought this child into the world.

In a few weeks, Annie was back at her post while Mom picked up raising Kelly, with the same dull pattern that she had provided for Annie. Now, she sits, drunken and disheveled in the back room of Jade's restaurant—lamenting her daughter.

As she sobered up, somewhat, BJ and Jade questioned her. Why didn't she report her daughter missing, where could she have gone, where did the finger come from? They bombarded her with questions beyond her current state and capability. People living in the Pines didn't interact much with authorities. But Annie was in no condition to provide hard answers through her drunken stupor and her grief.

Annie figured that her daughter had just hitched up with some trucker and headed south or west. That was until St. Nicholas Day, which fell on 5 December 1999. Many "real-world" customs were still practiced in the sparse houses scattered through the Pines. People put a shoe outside to receive a treat from St. Nicholas. It was usually a good treat. Annie's Mom continued this

35

tradition over the years. To placate her, Annie would put out the shoe and make sure to put a treat out for her growing-older-fast mother.

This December morning, she went out to put the treat in the shoe, and found the small decorated box that she had brought into the tavern. She couldn't believe her eyes. What did this mean? It was clearly Kelly's painted finger—or was it a crude trick from a neighbor? Over the next two weeks, between "tricks" and drunken stupors, Annie continued to ask around about Kelly's whereabouts. Her closest step to authority was her visit to Jade's tavern!

As Annie began to sober up, BJ and Jade pushed her for more information about her daughter.

Chapter 6
Annie's Daughter Kelly's Story

Almost sixteen years after her birth in 1982, "Princess" Kelly was recapturing the legend of Annie's career. Just one year ago, she had dropped out of Central Pines High. The regional school was not conducive to a warm interchange between students from highly diverse backgrounds. Central Pines had only been constructed in response to the introduction of gambling in Atlantic City. It became typical of the large impersonal high schools that dotted the major metropolitan areas in USA. It was not what Kelly expected living in the Pine Barrens.

The New Jersey legislature passed the initial bills for approval in 1974 and by 1978 the first Casino (Resorts) opened. Real estate brokers and land-sharks began to make way for the wave of employees that would relocate in Ocean County. Indeed, the face of South Jersey was about to change. By the 1980s, Central Pines was educating over 4,000 students in grades 9-12. They came from all over the region. As a result, Pineys and the Elite were all tossed into the public school mix (or mess, as some of them called it).

Kelly was as disinterested in school as her mother and this was even accentuated by the wide range of girls and boys who walked the halls of the huge complex. The school had become highly impersonal with students fending for themselves with the creation of cliques and "clubs" (sanctioned and unsanctioned).

Growing up among the rural pines was not easy for anyone—particularly the young beauty that Kelly was turning out to be. Adjusting to the school culture was even more difficult. She wasn't a cheerleader, nor was she a member of the marching band or honor society. She was certainly beautiful, but wandered rather faceless throughout the school. The best she got was the crude comments from some of the older boys and even the leering looks of some of the (rather handsome) members of the faculty.

During her last (sophomore) year, Kelly had become friendly with a few other girls from her area of the Pines. These girls spoke to her of a "cool club" that met at a variety of interesting places within the Pine Barrens. They spoke of mysterious initiation rites that new members had to follow. While a bit of this was intriguing for Kelly, she blew them off and went on her way. For the rest of her time at the school, these girls continue to cajole her about not joining the club. They almost became nasty about it…

Now, there was nothing keeping Kelly in that school, so she withdrew with little objections from her mother as soon as she turned 16. Annie was at a loss to provide her with guidance and no one in the school seemed to care! She simply became a dropout statistic.

Her early life memories were of a remote but warm shack in the woods. Her grandmother and grandfather seemed ancient to the little girl—until they just weren't there anymore. She had heard them speaking of much of the legend of the pine-barrens. The story of the Jersey Devil was told over and over again in front of a cold winter fire. She was also, always warned about not wandering too far from their little cabin. The little girl listened with some small degree of interest, but the small TV in the living room made for much of her early life.

Her first experience with other kids came with her entry to Kindergarten. The yellow bus picked her up on the corner of the road that her mother walked her to each morning. It became hard to make friends in this remote setting. As the socialization continued Kelly became the butt of jokes about her clothing and quiet—almost dumb-like demeanor. She made no real friends, sat alone in the lunchroom. Because she was quiet, she simply "fell through the cracks". She was no problem—therefore no true attention.

By the time Middle School came around, her developing feminine features began to gain attention from the overactive prepubescent boys, which didn't make her a fan of her female classmates. Although she didn't pay any real attention to the boys, that didn't help her social standing at all.

As she began to mature, she escaped into the glitz of her teen magazines and the magnetic lure of cable TV that had finally arrived—even in the beaten down shacks in the pine villages. By the time she reached high school, the stories of Atlantic City and the lure of the magazines and television drew Kelly in a removed, yet comfortable silent place. Her mom didn't know what to do with her, her grandparents were now gone.

It was one week after her 16th birthday she announced to her mother that she was quitting school. It was late in her sophomore year. Annie was disappointed but not shocked. She rather expected that Kelly could help take care of the house until she found some sort of work. Annie began to ask around to see what work her daughter might pick up.

By this time, Kelly knew about her mother's occupation, but Annie had never brought anyone to her shack, and that minimized the impact on Kelly. Her mother's night hours and provocative attire did not fool Kelly. In fact, it rather fascinated her.

Nevertheless, the Atlantic City that Kelly was about to discover was radically different from the one that her mother knew in her later years in the trade. Casinos had replaced conventions. New crowds of high rollers were enjoying the hey-day of the new AC. Annie's earlier profits had provided some small benefits from which Kelly could look out into the world—beyond the dull high school she had just left.

Her mother's early rude experiences helped protect Kelly from the brutal indignities—but she couldn't pull her from the draw of the trade. Kelly began to ask telling questions of Annie—mostly about sex. It became clearer and clearer to Annie that Kelly was looking to recreate her own profession. Annie was reluctantly resigned with Kelly's situation. She felt helpless yet tried to make the best of it. Lacking the sophisticated parental skills needed, she reached out for help to those people she knew best, her fellow whores!

Annie privately spoke to the group of girls who she still shared experiences with. One early afternoon, as the girls prepared for their nightly effort, she began to quietly cry. This led to her telling Kelly's story. Annie had a good generation on most of these women, and they had difficulty comprehending her situation. "You've got to promise to protect her," Annie cried. "We can't let her fall into the hands of the hardline pimps!"

Finally, after her tears and cajoling, she got her friends to promise to protect her and they truly pampered the girl, who was to become known as "Princess". They took these steps out of loyalty to Annie, whom they all respected.

Annie continue to tell her story as BJ and Jade sat transfixed at the figure of the aging prostitute who trembled as she continued to speak of her daughter.

"The last time I seen her was back in the summer," Annie continued as she mindlessly blew small smoke rings into the musty back room air. "We had been fightin' over money. I been taking care of it for all these years, partly since Dad died and Mom can't hardly do anything anymore. I guess I really didn't mind, too much, that Kelly worked the trade, but I was still always bitchin' at her to do better…I thought my pestering might just help her out of serious trouble, sweet thing that she was.

"Guess till today, I thought she'd just up and run off with one of those trucker fellas and head up to New York City. I never knew what happened to her when she went off—guess I'll never know now…"

****

It was in mid-July 1999 and Princess Kelly was still pissed at her mother as she sat in the back of the Greyhound bus that took her on the 25-minute trip into Atlantic City. "I'm making more than twice what that old bitch makes or ever made—and she's gonna tell me how to run my life," she fumed as she tucked her silk blouse into the short-tailored skirt she wore. Travelers sharing that ride into Atlantic City turned their heads to watch her—men and women alike. Dressed tastefully in in silk and heels, she looked like a misplaced young socialite of 23 rather than a boardwalk hooker. Princess had developed real class and she knew how to show it off.

The bus dropped her off at Trump's Taj and she walked the four blocks quickly to the main tourist entrance at Harrah's. Harrah's was one of the first of the casinos to open in AC, and many were quickly to follow. Many regulars began their search for Harrah's before heading out to other casinos. Because of her style, height, and regal bearing, Kelly never had a problem moving past the security people, most of whom she now knew by name, to work the crowd at the $50 minimum crap tables and at the surrounding bars. One of her mom's friends had steered her with this advice and Kelly was never disappointed.

Sometimes her john would take her up to a suite right there at Harrah's—on other occasions they went out, together, to other casinos and either stayed at one of them—or one of the many motels that populated the roads that led across the marshes and bays into the city. Either way, she brought in between $200-$600 an evening—a far cry from Annie's "wages" along route 9 and the Garden State Parkway.

This, however, was to be Kelly's last paycheck! It was early evening and a large crowd had formed around the crap table. A tall, distinguished man, who looked to be in around 50, was on a hot role. Dressed in jeans and a plain red t-shirt, he stood out from the jackets and ties that predominated at the high roller table. Plying her skills, Kelly eyed the pile of chips in front of him. Within a few hours, she became his "lucky charm". He cashed out and, arms intertwined, they headed out into the cool boardwalk air. He was staying at Caesars, just a few long blocks down from Harrah's.

He was balding slightly, but his remaining hair was nearly trimmed—with streaks of silver that set off piercing eyes that seemed far younger. They made love as soon as they got to his room. Kelly was strangely moved by his quiet and gentle lovemaking. This was not the typical grunt, moan, and squirt john that she normally serviced.

When they finished, he fixed drinks from the in-room bar and called for some thick sandwiches from room service. They talked long into the night. Usually, the men did all the talking, but this guy began encouraging Kelly to talk and to share her dreams. She thought he might be some kind of a teacher or professor?

She was shocked to find it was 4:00 AM. A normal three-trick night had been wasted on one nice older man. So nice that he offered to drive her across the inlet to the diner near her home. Somewhere in the recesses of her mind, a small quiet alarm should have been ringing. She thought she saw a strange cloud fall over the stranger's eyes as she spoke about her life. But the alarm was buried by the kindness with which he enveloped her. He handed her five crisp hundred-dollar bills, as they climbed into the cab of his shiny new truck and headed out across the marshland to a diner that Kelly usually frequented.

Kelly asked to get out near a cross road about a quarter mile from the diner. He kissed her gently on the cheek as she climbed sown and Kelly thought she saw a small tear break the piercing depth of his eye. She wasn't sure if she could hear his car tires spin into the highway as she quietly walked back on the shoulder of the road. She quietly walked down the shoulder of the road toward the diner where some of her fellow-hooker friends would be having an early morning coffee. She heard some laughter and movement behind her as she entered the all night facility. At 4:30 AM, none of her friends were there! A familiar waitress poured her a steaming cup of black coffee.

As she waited for her coffee to cool, she heard the door open and a small group of people walked in. She didn't know any of them. They seemed to be eyeing her up, but she was relatively used to that. It was a group of about seven people of mixed ages. Some appeared to be teens and a few were clearly adults. A few of the younger girls seemed familiar to Kelly. Perhaps they were some of the crew who taunted her at Central Pines?

Two of the adults were in business suits and the teens seemed to have a hodgepodge of different style closes, hair colors, and piercings. They sat down at a table and ordered a breakfast. The older gentlemen, dark complected, seemed to be in charge, he had an old-fashioned hat that covered much of his face. He was clearly in charge!

Kelly was feeling uncomfortable in their presence. The two girls she thought she knew must have known her. They combined snarls, snickered together and laughed in her direction. Kelly thought they might have been a part of the Cheerleading squad. She started to walk over toward them—but had second thoughts. What could be gained from a conflict at 4:30 AM? She threw down two dollars, said thanks to the waitress and headed out the door. The young girls seemed to turn as she departed for home.

She was only several blocks from her mom's home in the pines. Her mind was barraged the images of the man she met this evening combined with the strange group that just walked into the diner. She thought she heard some quiet talking behind her. She stopped and quickly turned, but saw nothing. Kelly continued down the dark street.

She picked up her walking pace, but her high heels deterred her pace. She began to hear footsteps quickly catching up with her. She never heard the strange sounds that crept up behind her. The last thing she felt was a sudden intense pain that radiated down her spine. It felt like a cold steel blade had impaled the smooth white skin that separated her spinal column from the elements. But that was her last feeling as she slipped into unconsciousness.

Chapter 7
Identifying the Body

Gleeson sat mesmerized through Annie's long story. His love of history had driven him back from the baseball diamond to school teaching. He had spent several years in North Jersey before he relocated after his pending divorce. He had been enthralled as a young man with stories about the Jackson Whites in North Jersey. They were a mixture of Revolutionary Deserters from both sides, some of them Dutch, and runaway slaves. Stories like these led BJ into a fascination with local history. Now he was being drawn into the very strange history of this part of his State!

Annie's problem triggered his inquisitive nature and he pulled Jade to the side: "We should try to help her, she needs us. Let me take Annie and try to find out what's happening here. It's the beginning of my Christmas vacation and I'm bored anyway."

BJ further offered to take Annie around to some of the rural and/or state police to find any evidence of Kelly. Jade was a bit reticent to get this much involved. After all, they had to deal with drunks at closing time on too many occasions. But she could see that BJ really seemed to care for Annie—so she conceded to BJ's wish. Jade put Annie up on a cot in a spare room in the back and told her BJ would be there to pick her up in the morning.

Gleeson drove quietly through the empty streets, winding his way to his small apartment. His mind wandered with the stories that he had heard from Annie this evening. BJ returned, late, to his pad and began to look through the notes he had been taking on local history. Books were filled with strange and frequently unbelievable stories about this part of the state.

The people of the Pine Barrens had a truly unique history. Stories of the Jersey devil, Indian rituals, and revolutionary war games flowed through his notes. Could any of this have to do with Annie and her daughter? Probably not;

however, that interesting symbol seemed somewhat familiar. Where had he seen it before? He poured himself a small jigger of his evening favorite, Irish whiskey, while he continued to scour the Internet and his notes.

His alarm went off at 8:00 AM and he staggered out of bed. He was surprised that he hadn't gotten back to his apartment until 4:40 AM! He splashed water over his face, took a quick shower, and decided to head out to pick up Annie.

On Tuesday, Annie had sobered up when BJ showed up at the tavern to pick her up. She was still disconsolate over the disappearance of her daughter and the discovery of the finger. She had discovered the small box just in front of the door of her shack in the woods. She insisted on carrying that box on her possession. Apparently after finding the box, she had apparently just wandered around from rural tavern to store, asking about Kelly and getting progressively drunker—showing the gruesome product to anyone who would look.

Jade and Annie were sitting at the same table in the back of the bar over mugs of coffee and a pile of sweet rolls. "Any of those for me?" BJ hadn't had any breakfast so he sat down to join them. He worried if he should bring Annie on his search, but know that he couldn't identify the body—even if they even found one. Jade had arranged to take the day off, so that made BJ feel just a little bit better about their venture for the day. He found her presence quietly peaceful.

They piled into BJ's van and began to head out on the back highways of central-south Jersey. Jade had located several state police barracks. They had a road map and they began to approach them one-by-one. Hard questions to ask! Annie hadn't filed any missing person's report, so they were left to just asking about unclaimed bodies: Found any bodies lately? Especially pretty girls missing a finger!

No matter how they asked the questions, they received rather quizzical almost amusing responses. While the officers were all polite and respectful, BJ could tell that they were not particularly invested in helping with this problem. The barracks are reasonably scattered among the back highways and they had stopped at three places until he finally got a response.

Finally, they reached one particular station that looked like military barracks, actually located right on the Garden State Parkway, and BJ asked the same question, fully expecting the same answers. He left Jade and Annie in the car as he had done in the other stops.

At this station, the desk officer scratched his head, said he thought they might have something, and walked inside to get his lead officer. A greying, near-retirement Captain came out from his office to meet BJ. Annie had filled out a form with Kelly's description that BJ had in his possession. The officer asked him to sit down and BJ recognized that the officer had something!

"We don't have anything directly meeting her description, but back last summer, during a traffic jam up in Swedesboro, on 322, one of my troopers was directed to the site of a badly disfigured, partially decomposed, and battered body on the side of the road."

The Captain paused, then continued: "It was difficult to determine a cause of death, due to the damage the body had received on the road over the previous night. We are not sure how long the remains were laying there. There were also some missing limbs, probably pulled off by some scavenging animals in the area. We do even have some wolves and coyotes down here. We might be able to get you some assistance if you can bear with us for an hour or so."

Gleeson thought this might be worth bringing Annie in. "Annie, they have a possible lead on what might have happened to Kelly, we need to go inside for a bit." Annie began to tremble. Gleeson helped her out of the car and the three of them re-entered that station.

"This is the missing person's mother. I am here on her behalf; I need to help her with her search. Is there somewhere we can sit down?" They left Annie and Jade on the bench as Gleeson and the Officer walked to a back office.

"I don't know why you want to be involved in this?" said the officer quietly.

"Well, officer, Annie can't help herself, and I'm feeling somewhat responsible for her once she walked into my girlfriend's bar."

The Captain was giving Annie a strange look. He finally asked her, "Do I know you from somewhere?"

Annie didn't know how to answer. She was tired and frustrated with the day so far: "Maybe you busted me in the Atlantic City area?" As the Captain hesitated and turned back, Annie whispered under her breath to BJ, "He might have been one of my clients!"

BJ spoke to him as he seemed to be walking away, "Let me see if you can help. Is there a way you can direct us?"

"Mr.," the Captain replied, "I don't even know if there are any remains kept over this period of time. Here is my card, my name is Captain Greg Barlow, feel free to keep me posted on whatever you discover." BJ walked Jade and Annie back out to the car. Annie continued to shake with fear. Jade was trying to comfort her. BJ was a bit aggravated with the behavior of the Captain but he went back into the barracks to press the matter a bit.

Very reluctantly, the Captain directed BJ to the area morgue with a letter of entry. At BJ's request, he also gave him the name of one of his Officers who could be his contact moving forward. The closest working morgue was in Millville so they needed to head back about an hour away from the tavern. Unidentified or unclaimed "suspicious" corpses in this entire area are routinely sent to this facility.

The barrack center they had visited didn't routinely see anything like this and there was no uproar to solve a crime—if there is one. This could have been a wandering drunk who got smashed on the shoulder and battered up over the night.

"Send it off to Millville, unless someone claims the body"—that was this rural station's standard modes operandi. But four months had passed and there was no real sense of urgency to answer the concerns of an old drunken woman! BJ and Jade were trying to change that.

Annie was a real mess by now as he led her back to his car. But she was appreciative of their attention to her. She whimpered quietly as they drove about 30 miles to Millville Hospital, which housed the area morgue. Their stated purpose was to identify a body. Their true purpose was to simply find out what had happened to Kelly!

They waited impatiently for over an hour. Annie's condition was worsening by the minute. Finally, a woman in a white coat came out to see them. She was obviously a part of the coroners department. Gleeson produced his letter of entry that the State Police had provided and the woman in attendance scratched her head.

"I'm not sure what you are looking for. The only bodies we have here have only been here 2-3 days and don't match the young woman you were looking for. But we do have one area labeled as UUC!" BJ made a quizzical face. "Sorry Sir, that stands for 'unidentified and unrecognizable corpses'. This is reserved for bodies found for which there is no identification and little means of physical identification. We maintain them for 12 months before depositing

46

them in a community grave at the local cemetery. It is a pretty gruesome collection, in case you REALLY want to look."

BJ reluctantly shook his head "yes" and they moved to a basement area of the building. This time they needed to bring Annie with them. It was poorly lighted with several small containers set in a refrigerated wall. Each box had a date written on the outside. BJ saw one marked 8-23-1998. Annie had said that Kelly disappeared sometime before Labor Day. "Let me take a look at that box, please."

It was a gruesome sight—there was barely enough to recognize humanity. No full skull, teeth, fingers for prints…just a rough pile of remaining body parts and tethered clothing. But long hair and two tattoos were still visible on a portion of arm and what resembled a human back. The problem with the arm was that there was no hand attached. BJ looked closely and it appeared to have been severed. The tattoos were identical, each were tricolored (blue, red, and green) circles with a crude brown cross in the center.

Annie was standing back, with Jade's arm around her. BJ asked Jade to bring her forward. Annie saw those, "that's my Kelly," she screamed plaintively, and promptly passed out again. The attendant escorted them back to the main waiting area while they treated Annie. Gleeson stood in the hallway pondering the next steps. He pulled the note that the Captain had given him for an additional contact. BJ decided to call—immediately.

An officer answered: "Officer Collins here, how can I help you?"

"Thanks Officer Collins, my name is BJ Gleeson, I was just speaking with your Captain about a missing person case."

"Yes, he just told me he gave my information to several people who came here together looking for a young girl."

"Well, we just found her," said BJ. "I'll be in touch with Captain Barlow to see how we can proceed with this case."

"I'll be glad to be of assistance," replied Collins.

BJ was going to try to look deeper into the situation. What had happened to poor Kelly on those last days of August? Something was gnawing at the recesses of his mind as he thought about his next steps. Why was he so interested in Annie? Was he trying to get closer to Jade through Annie? Or was it just his personal quiet historical obsession with the history of this strange area?

Annie was somewhat better now—but still in a state of semi-shock. They put her in the van and headed back to Staley's. She moaned quietly over another cup of coffee. "My Kelly, My Kelly…" over and over again. It was a pathetic sight. Jade decided to let Annie stay in the extra room she had over the tavern—to keep an eye on her.

BJ made a call to Barlow and Collins to inform them that they had identified Kelly's body. They agreed to meet within a week or so to review whatever next steps need to be taken in an odd situation like this. Barlow sounded very supportive over the phone. As BJ hung up, he had a flash back from a recent historical note he had read about the Pines… He was going to have to dig into his historical notes again. But for now, they needed to get Annie back to the tavern.

Gleeson got Jade and Annie back to the tavern before 4 PM. He helped Jade get Annie settled into a room above the tavern. She was fading fast after the traumatic discovery of the past hour. BJ waited at the bar until Jade came down. He realized he was famished so he ordered an early supper of Fish and Chips. Jade sat down next to him as he ate.

"What do we do next, BJ?"

"Well, I need to get back with the state police to see what they recommend. I think for now we just have to support Annie and help her get back on her feet. Hearing Annie's story of Kelly's life, I think there are a few more avenues to explore: her clients…her school friends."

"BJ, be careful, you're no detective."

"Yes, but I care and I have a good deal of experience in historical research that might just give me some help in solving a real problem," BJ said. "Besides, that should give me some real 'creds' as I try to find out what happened to that girl! Like you well know, I am easily bored; this gives me an opportunity to involve my investigative skills into something productive.

"But right now I have to get out of here, I need some fresh air to clear my brain! I'm heading down to the shore, wanna join me?"

Jade responded, "It's going to get busy soon for supper, I'll see if I can shake loose and join you later."

"OK, I'm heading to Whale Beach…" said BJ.

Chapter 8
Whale Beach

Whale Beach was a remote portion of the Jersey Shore. It was technically in the village of Strathmere, which bordered both Sea Isle City and Upper Township. Only about 150 people inhabited this small strip of land throughout the year. This grew to several thousand vacationers each summer in the 400 residences on the island.

It is technically named Ludlam Island and was settled initially by a branch of the Lenape Indians who inhabited that area. BJ couldn't think of a better place to escape to, particularly in the winter. He parked his van near a sand dune and walked through the divider down into the open beach area. It was just beginning to get dark as he headed down toward the water.

Where was he going, what was he doing with his life? What does this incident with Annie have to do with the life-path he was on? (These are the kind of reflections that he allowed himself as he wandered along the quiet waves of low tide.) BJ thought he had found pay dirt in Sea Isle City, but his wanderings and discovery of Whale Beach had provided him with a whole new perspective on "thinking by the sea".

He thought about this new career that was opening for him at Central Pines. He reflected on Matthews, his old, kinda friend and new leader. He thought about the other characters that made up the faculty. Did he really have a future here—at the school, or with Jade? Probably the next few years would open up a true-life path for Gleeson. Would he enjoy life as a school administrator? Was that what he really wanted?

But what had he gotten himself into? He was now driving all over the state with Jade and an old woman, searching for her believed-dead daughter. He knew he was a historian, but he regretted that he was not possessed with a great memory. He had to hunt, save his information, and write it down. This was proving to be his strength, however, as that provided him a base to move back to as he continued his search. His life path was also considerably based on his own faith walk and personal "study".

He was strengthened by the old testament book of Jeremiah (Chapter 29: Verse 11): "For I know the plans I have for you, says the Lord, Plans for good and not for evil, to give you a hope and a future." That thought was guiding him through this new part of his life's journey. But as he read further, he hit verse 13 that reminded him that these great plans only happen when "you will seek me and find me when you seek me with all your heart". Where was his heart?

Was he too wrapped up in his career at the expense of his family and his relationships? He thought about his children, his ex, his Baseball Team, his school career. Now Annie had entered the picture, but his thoughts kept coming back to Jade. In the middle of his morass of life she was becoming a point of calm and peace. He was beginning to wonder what real love is all about—besides sex. He only knew that when Jade was with him, he was at true peace—no matter what else was going on around them.

As he walked, his mind moved back to the origins of the beach he now walked upon. What other footprints in the sand have been erased over the centuries. He thought initially of the Lenape who fished these waters and hunted these pines. He thought of the impact on those people who have lived in the Pine Barrens for generations. He stopped to pick up another large shell. He often found these on Whale Beach.

There was a time when whales actually washed up on these shores. Indians probably used their carcasses for a variety of purposes. Scientists now studied these remains to reflect on ecological issues.

But then his image shifted to the washed up body of Kelly lying in that icebox morgue in Millville. Something deep inside BJ cried out for justice as much on behalf of Annie as for her now deceased daughter. As he walked that beach, he resolved to use all of his skills and intelligence to try to solve the puzzle of a girl he had never met brutal death.

His cell phone was vibrating in his pocket. He had forgotten to turn it on fully. He looked at the area code (201) and realized it was his ex-wife, Cassie, or his daughter. He pressed the answer button.

"Benjamin," a stern voice answered. He now knew it was his ex for she was the only one that called him by his given name! In addition, she did that when she was angry. So he prepared for an attack.

"You are entitled to forget that you once had a wife, but that doesn't excuse you from forgetting that you have two children!" she chided.

BJ figured this was coming. In truth, he had been so involved with his relocation he had failed to keep up with his two children. But after all, they were grown now and on their own. As he thought that, he realized he was rationalizing. Children are always your children, and your ex-wife will always be the mother of those children.

"Happy almost New Year to you too," said BJ sarcastically. What a way to start a conversation!

"Don't give me any of that crap, this is about your daughter!"

"I'm sorry, Cassie, I was lost in thought, what's up with Carly?"

"Nothing, yet, but you know she's fresh out of college and trying to find her place in life. I am doing my best to help her out—but she is still hurting emotionally—she needs her dad—more frequently." Cassie had forged a productive career for herself in the advertising industry. She now commuted to NYC to work in one of the larger houses there. Fortunately, that saved BJ on any alimony payments for the divorce.

"And James is doing quite well, raking in the legal funds in Missouri, but you need to own up to the emotional needs of both of them. You are too much about yourself these last few months."

BJ realized she was on a rant that would not go away soon. He tried to sooth her while at the same time recognizing many of his own shortcomings as a husband and a father. "You're right, Cassie, what can I do for either of them, or for you for that matter? We did 'make those kids' together and I am thankful to you for the mother you were for them.

"Cassie, what do you suggest I do, you know I am just getting on my feet down here?"

"For one thing, call both of them a lot more frequently. A birthday card or a Christmas gift is not a match for talking and, more importantly spending time together. Would you PLEASE see if you could take care of that?"

BJ settled himself. He sat down on a nearby bench. He took a deep breath and sighed, "Cassie, you're right, I have screwed up with you, Carly and James in the past. I'll see what I can do with both of them. Are you all OK?"

"Like I said," Cassie continued, "I know there is a real gap between you and your son. James is great but I know he's got some issues with our divorce that you both need to work out. He is a busy professional but you need to find the time; but Carly is another story. She is looking into entering a graduate program to become a physician's assistant. She'll be living in Delaware and serving an internship in that area. She has found an apartment that I am helping her with. She is just plain lonely and you've not spent much time with her. Please see what you can do for both of them."

"Cassie, I will call them both tomorrow and try to set up some time with Carly in the next few weeks. Please keep me in your prayers, if not your heart, because I need God's help with my continued journey."

"Take care of yourself," said Cassie as she hung up.

He was beginning to put his thoughts in order after that difficult call when he realized that he was walking too far down on the beach. His cell phone hummed, again, in his pocket. He hesitated to answer but this time it was Jade.

"Where are you, I am up by the Boardwalk and 12th St., are you still at the beach?" His mood brightened immediately as he gave her directions where they could meet. As he walked back towards the boardwalk, he noted her long hair, in the sea breeze, as she came walking down the steps onto the beach area.

They briefly embraced and joined hands as they ambled toward Atlantic City along the ocean water line. In spite of the romance of the evening, both of them were drawn to the situation facing Annie. They realized that they had been drawn into a situation neither of them was really able to handle. Yet here they were in the middle of a tragic death. It got both their minds off their own personal family struggles and enabled them to share thoughts toward a solution to a messy affair.

BJ had no idea where to get started, but he agreed that he was out of school until 4 January, since New Year's Day (The Millennial!) was on Sunday, school would not resume until the following Wednesday. He told Jade he would be able to do some amateur detective work over that next week. Jade agreed that she would stay close to Annie to see what else she could find out. Also, her daughter went to the same high school that Kelly had attended, so Jade said she would see what her daughter, Justine, knew—if anything—about her.

All of a sudden, Gleeson stopped short. "We're walking too far North...time to head back..." The lights in Atlantic City were beginning to look a little bigger. Jade laughed, reached up and kissed him gently on the lips. BJ returned the kiss with even more ardor as they stood in the sand. When they finally got back to their respective cars, they embraced for a final kiss before heading off in their different directions.

For a while, BJ just sat in his van reflecting on the long day. The phone call from Cassie, difficult as it was, reminded him of better days. He could not ignore or forget his children while he moved into this new place of life. His mind was racing through the events of the past two days trying to put together some semblance of a plan.

He realized that even though Jade's daughter was in the high school, BJ could go into the school—check out some records. He would use his newfound friendship with Principal Matthews to see if he can help him find more information on Kelly while she was at the high school. And how would he get time to meet with his daughter during all of this?

He was also painfully conscious of his own weak spots. He seemed to have a combination of several "maladies" which pursued him throughout his life. Some of his tendencies bordered on OCD (obsessive compulsive disorder). Even now he was focusing almost too carefully and intently on some of the events and people that he was encountering. Added to that, he had earlier been diagnosed in middle school as ADHD (Attention Deficit Hyperactivity Disorder). Fortunately, he never was put on Ritalin, but he struggled just the same.

He always had to be "doing something". This is what initially got him into trouble with the sexuality of the Internet. It was there, cheap and ready for instant gratification. BJ was becoming aware that he could utilize these ailments to help him focus on the problem that was confronting Annie at this time. This could work to her advantage. In addition, he was hoping that this would him out of this morass of life that he currently found himself in.

Would he be able to channel his hyperactivity and inquisitive nature into a positive outcome through this present situation? He was certainly finding a sense of satisfaction as he became more involved with Kelly's story. He felt an internal sense of confidence that he could truly make a difference. He had quickly lost that in professional baseball and he hadn't quite found it yet in teaching—but could he blend those experiences into a new direction for himself. He needed something!

He slowly pulled out of the parking lot and weaved through the streets of Sea Isle to his apartment. It had been a long and possibly productive day!

Chapter 9
The Diary of Sir Guy Carlton – June 1772

Gleeson got back to his apartment around 10 PM. He realized he had forgotten to eat so he threw together some pasta and used his trusty microwave to un-freeze meatballs and sat down to his exquisite Italian supper. This should tide him over! He poured a small measure of Irish whiskey (neat) and kicked back at his desk. Gleeson had rediscovered several pieces of literature relative to the history of the Pine Barrens. He wasn't quite sure each of them would help, but it certainly helped him clear his mind.

It was a series of pages from a dairy of a revolutionary war soldier. BJ was reminded of a recent outing he had at a small golf course off Route 9, just outside of Atlantic City. He was playing by himself, as he often does to clear his head. It was a small course between Route 9 and the Bay. On the fifth hole, he hit an errant ball, as he often does, into the woods. He thought he would take a quick look for the ball in case it was in the clear.

As he walked through the trees, he saw what appeared to be some very old tombstones! He read the inscriptions and found that they were all dated in the late 1700s. He picked up his ball and headed back to finish the course.

When he was done, he asked the owner about the odd cemetery. It turns out that it was a revolutionary war cemetery that has been preserved; he had to agree to build his small course around the "scene". He claimed that a local historical group came in to keep it clean once a month.

He knew that there had been some activity in South Jersey between New York and Philadelphia, but never knew the extent until he uncovered this diary in one of the area historical centers. BJ had never really considered the presence of the Revolutionary War in this part of the state! The local historical group was only too happy to share copies of some original journals they had in their possession.

Sir Guy looked back at the five rag-tag soldiers that followed him along the banks of the slow-moving river. One member of their small group had a musket ball imbedded in his lower leg and the other men had to help him. This slowed their journey considerably. Just up ahead he could see the tall pines fanning back and exposing a clear sandy beach and a large open expanse of choppy water. Here they could stop, pitch quarters and determine their route for the next day.

Three months earlier and forty-five miles north, an obscure incident at the fringe of the American Revolution had made these men refugees. In April, a continental soldier named Joshua Huddy was hanged to death by loyalist forces in Toms River, NJ as a reward for his brave resistance against a British contingent a month earlier.

Carlton knew Huddy, but even though they were on opposite sides, Carlton's needed to escape the rivalry of this present conflict. He knew from the trappers and inland explorers, that America offered tranquil settings in their vast wilderness. New beginnings could be found by heading west. He picked up a few other men who shared his beliefs, packed minimal provisions, and began moving at daybreak.

They were now officially deserters—hunted by the Continental Army and moving under the pain of hanging from their own British Officers. They had a brief skirmish with some colonial revolutionaries as they moved through the area. That's how they ended up with one wounded man.

Initially, the group planned on heading south to the Delaware River and then moving westward. Armed with a few skills for survival and limited to first-hand accounts, they triggered all their adrenaline for their quest to escape. None of the six men had any family in the colonies. All of them were at risk for their lives when the revolutionary forces concluded their victories. They were hopeful that friendly natives populated this pine region and that they could eventually live peacefully among them, before moving on to the more established settlements in the West. They certainly would not be welcomed back in England.

As they came to the edge of the great harbor, Carlton and his men saw a wide river seemed to weave its broad body back for miles through the Western pines. Tired from their twelve-hour march, they sucked up their energies to plod inland along the new river for about an hour before setting camp. Tracks and spent fires gave evidence of recent dwellers.

They knew that Indians, generally peaceful, occupied many of these areas—and hoped they might encounter some. As they moved about a mile upriver, they came upon a deserted lean-to and Carlton declared the first day flight at an end. They unpacked their simple possessions and prepared for a fire while Carlton and his lieutenant, Potter, loaded their muskets and headed back into the thick pine cove in hopes of fresh venison to accompany the dried beef they had brought along. The sound of musket fire range out loudly and echoed across the vast Pine Barrens. In less than an hour—Carlton and Potter returned with a small buck, ready for the fire.

The men ate ravenously, sucked hard on their small supply of rum and fell-bloated, and bone-tired into a deep sleep, interrupted by dreams of their future and nightmares of their escaped past.

Carlton woke with a start at daybreak. He thought he heard stirrings in the surrounding woods. He pulled on his boots and headed out to scout the area. He moved quietly through the trees surrounding their encampment. All of a sudden he noticed several natives moving stealthily through the trees, toward the remaining men, who were still sleeping.

At first, Carlton wanted to confront the natives, but something told him to stand quiet. He watched in quiet horror as the natives moved swiftly toward the five sleeping men. They first dragged off the wounded soldier. Next they stood of the remaining men up and moved them to the center of the encampment. They quickly, and rather efficiently, slit the throat of each man.

Fresh blood spilled over the hard ground. They then put the bodies together and began to perform some sort of ritual over the bodies. They then cut down some limbs and formed a crude cross in the center of the encampment. They dragged the wounded soldier to the center and fastened him to the cross. They proceeded to burn him alive, chanting to some God Carlton had never heard about. As Carlton watched he noted that each native had a strange three—colored marking, in the form of a cross, on his or her chest and right forearm.

To his further horror, he saw the group now step back from the remaining bodies. They were holding up the severed left hand of each man. They looked around and quietly slid back into the wood from whence they had come! Carlton was rattled beyond belief; his concepts of the 'peaceful native' were shaken in an instance. "Was this typical," he thought, "or some bizarre exception to the rule?"

Carlton began to move swiftly and quietly in the opposite direction. He knew he was heading west. Around noon of his first journey day, he came upon a number of rough-hewn cabins sitting almost in the midst of a group of Pine Trees. Several people slowly walked out into the center of the homes as he entered the area. They didn't appear to be Native Americans, their skin colors ranged from brown through red brown, coffee…

One, rather large, young, man stepped forward brandishing a musket—similar to those seen by Carlton in earlier battles. The man was taller than Carlton and had a strange hue about him. His was Albino, and his eyes were a piercing blue. His hair was tightly curled upon his head. He spoke English!

"What brings you to this part of the woods (in clear crisp English)?" said the man.

Carlton didn't want to rouse the man to anger. He almost wanted to ask the man how he had gotten to these parts. He wondered what he had walked into. He had some experiences with Black people in the New England area when he first arrived—but these folks were very different. He thought he might as well tell the truth since these people.

"To tell you God's truth, I am a runaway British soldier. My men have been slaughtered. I am on my way to the West. Technically, I am a 'deserter'! I am truly at your mercy here."

The tall man smiled at Carlton and invited him to stay through the evening and take food with them. Carlton experienced a warmth and understanding that he could not, at first, understand.

Surprisingly, most of the small 'tribe' seemed to be able to speak English. They allowed him to share their supper of fresh venison and some herbs and vegetables that had been picked fresh from a small garden he would see on the property.

As they sat and ate, a few of the people began to share their experiences with Carlton about their experiences. This group, of about thirty people had been originally located in Northern New Jersey; they had lived in those woods of the Ramapo Mountains. They had relocated to this place some ten years ago.

The growing tensions between the Native Americans and the budding state of revolution began to make their situation rather intolerable. It seems that they were mostly comprised of runaway slaves and indentured servants. They had been joined in the last few years with some Hessian deserters. Finally as the war heated up in that part of the state, they decided to pick up and relocate further south. Some former slaves from this part of the state had joined them as well.

Carlton felt comfortable in their midst. It was good to know that he wasn't the only one "escaping". He slept soundly on a blanket in the cabin of the man who appeared to be their leader. He headed out quietly in the morning, thanking the leader as he left.

In a day's time, he reached the Delaware River and encountered a peaceful tribe of natives. Eventually he found his way into West Virginia where he eventually migrated into the American South-West. Only he lived to tell the tale of that adventure.

****

The historical journal continued but BJ put the journal down. He was brought back to the junction points of 1782 and 1999. He had also read about similar rituals described between the Native American's from this region. The similarities, with the tattoos that matched those on Kelly, to the bizarre rituals that seemed to be a part of the lore of these pine barrens. How did those tattoos become so identical? What did they mean?

Also, it was also interesting to read about the presence of Blacks in the Pines. Gleeson might have been a washed up ball-player, high school teacher, and history nerd…but the sight of this poor woman was pushing him further into that inquisitive nature within him, that often got him in trouble in his life. Jade's compassion for old Annie was touching, and at this moment, Gleeson decided he was going to seriously commit to finding out what happened to her!

He had some time on his hands just now—and did he ever hate to be bored (part of his ADHD)! The police didn't seem to care much about a dead hooker (but he sure did), and it was late December, the middle of the Christmas Vacation. He had no real home to return to, so maybe he could figure this out before it was time to return to school in January. At this point, he was still enjoying his interactions with his new (but old) boss: Principal Clarke Matthews.

Chapter 10
Clarke Matthews' Early Life

Here he was back to work again, with the guy he had encountered when he first entered the educational arena as a substitute teacher during his off-season!

The school principal was an interesting guy, also with a background in North Jersey. Although he didn't have a full time job in education until he came down to South Jersey, BJ had worked for him for a while in Jersey City as a full-time substitute when he came back from the baseball season.

Matthews had been caught in an affair with one of the English teachers. That wouldn't have been too bad, but the woman in question was married to one of the board members. Bright, black, handsome, and highly articulate—couldn't quite save him. One day when he came in to substitute, he was shocked to see that Matthews had been fired.

Now BJ was job hunting in Southern New Jersey. He always loved the shore and hoped to be able to sink new roots there. He was surprised to see Matthews listed as Principal in the ad that had appeared for both a teaching and coaching position. He was equally surprised to hear Matthew's voice on the telephone when he called to invite BJ for an interview. It eased BJ's interviewing nerves as he sat and met with Matthews and his vice-principal, an older dude named "Doc" Martin.

"What would make you think to come down to these beautiful Pine Barrens?" began Matthews as the interview commenced. "You're a Northern Boy!"

BJ spent some time speaking of his final years in Baseball combined with his love for history and working with young people. He also alluded to his marital break-up since he thought Matthews might be somewhat sensitive and supportive of his situation.

"Well, you will find the students here very different from those of Jersey City. We do have quite a mixture of different types of families and kids. BJ, this position will involve teaching 11th and 12th grade United States History, but we also have a head Baseball Coach Position available. Still interested?"

BJ almost jumped out of his chair with enthusiasm. "I believe I can make a difference in the lives of these kids in both positions, given the chance."

BJ had close to a three-hour drive back to his temporary bachelor pad in Hackensack, so he had lots of time to think about the move. He had a few interviews in the shore area, but no real offers yet. It was getting too close to the new school year. As a result, he was surprised to receive a telephone call the very next day. Matthew's assistant principal, "Doc" Martin was calling to provide BJ with the news that his name was to be presented to the board of education for appointment that following day.

The job was his—if he wanted it. And, boy, did BJ want this chance. This opened up a bright opportunity for him to transition from his personal and professional past and to find a fresh start in the heart of the Pine Barrens.

Principal Clarke Matthews had an undergraduate degree from Yale and was a recent graduate of the doctoral program at Columbia. He had been raised in the Deep South but a fine scholarship turned him into a northerner. He didn't speak much about his background or his family—if he even had one! He was a bit of a quiet mystery man. But combined with his great personality, charm and charisma he drew the attention of both men and women alike.

In all of his schools, he worked hard to be "one of the boys" even though he was vastly different from most of his staff. The affair in Jersey City had sent ripples of additional rumors throughout the school – even before Matthews had announced his resignation. There were stories of drug usage and alcohol abuse. He was known to have a good bottle of Black Rum in his desk that he pulled out for his closest executive team members. No one was sure if he had been married once or twice but there were no signs or mentions of any of these women—or any children.

He enjoyed treating his close team and other school friends to an occasional Friday night out. It was during these occasions that after a few drinks, he would open up and spin off a variety of interesting tales about the deep south and his experience in the Caribbean Islands. A mixture of legends and, perhaps, exaggerations about places none of his new inner circle had ever experienced. They were forced to take their boss as his word.

He reintroduced this Friday concept once he got to Pineland Regional. He was both generous and likeable, with a sometime bizarre sense of humor. He had dubbed the get-together as the "Poets Club". One of the older teachers in the English Department was impressed and applauded his literary efforts. She realized she had not been invited to join. Then she found out the POETS stood for "Piss On Education Tomorrow's Saturday". That did not fly well with the veteran staff members.

Truth be known: Matthews had a more mysterious past then most people guessed. His actual roots were deep in the South. His great grandparents had roots as ex-slaves and sharecroppers on a Rice Plantation just South of Myrtle Beach in South Carolina. That plantation was taken over, long after slavery, by wealthy New Yorkers, and exists under the name "Brookgreen Gardens".

Clarke was raised on that former plantation property, now an exquisite sculptor part for tourists. He moved through the segregated schools of the South quite successfully. As soon as he left high school, with a full scholarship to Yale, he "ditched" his heritage and took on all the tones of a gentlemen who grew up in upper Harlem. He couldn't deny his 'blackness' but he worked hard to ignore his roots. He totally lost his Southern drawl.

After his advanced degree work, he seldom spoke about growing up in that area of South Carolina. He rather focused on the brash, bright college students that had taken over at Yale. His early upbringing was just a bit of a mystery that he never really alluded to. No talk of his father or his grandparents.

How he landed in the Pinelands was an equal mystery. Apparently, he had hired a public relations firm to washout his prior problems in North Jersey. He left Jersey City in 1996 to accept the new position and he had effectively left his reputation behind when he moved south. As the only black administrator at Pinelands, he found himself in a rather lonely leadership position. But he was quite used to that.

As a bright student, he had quickly moved into the ranks of the educational elite—that were mostly white. He skillfully manipulated his unique culture and background to his advantage. Clarke had a quiet allure that tended to impress the ladies and even—to some extent to the female staff and students at the school.

The interview between BJ and Matthews had been truly unique. BJ was surprised to find him in the Pinelands—but Matthews seemed to be very comfortable to reunite with his former teacher from the North.

When they met after his formal board appointment, Matthews spoke clearly to BJ: "BJ, it seems that both of us have brought some baggage with us to the Pinelands. Can we really talk? I do believe that we can develop some special magic here. You don't want to be a baseball coach and teacher forever—now do you?"

"Why not? I'm just looking for a fresh start here. I'm trying to put my life back together, and this seems like a good place to start," said BJ.

"I'm going to need another assistant principal in another year. I would like to move you into that spot so that I can then have you take over for me."

"Why do you want to put that on me?"

"I always some you to have some special empathy toward people that can be helpful in an administrative role. In addition, you bring some special background with your baseball experiences and your deep knowledge of history that can be parlayed into a great asset for this school in this part of the state."

BJ was taken back and somewhat flattered. He would now have a chance to rehabilitate himself into a leadership future. Just a few courses would allow him to move into this new position.

"Thanks for having such faith in me."

"Let's leave our pasts behind us and bring this school out of the Pines and into the 21st century," boasted Clarke.

BJ left the office somewhat stunned. He just wanted to be a history teacher and a coach and now Matthews was pushing him into an administrative role after only a brief experience with him in the earlier district. It was clear—without words—that BJ would keep his mouth shut about Matthews earlier career.

Once BJ began working in the school, however, it became clear that Matthews had a very small and close cadre of followers—both teachers and administrators. There was a quiet invisible barrier that seemed to separate that small group from the rest of the staff. BJ was being invited to join that inner circle. He wasn't quite sure why?

Matthews gave him a glowing introduction when the staff returned that August. He immediately began to take BJ under his wing and bring him into the meetings with this close-knit team. BJ was quickly invited to join the Friday POETS club.

The school had only been in existence since the late 70s and, itself, had a rather new and somewhat "checkered" existence. It was a product of the Casino growth in the area that resulted in quickly overcrowding what was initially a beautiful new school among the pines. Early school leadership represented the old guard of conservative education.

Former football coaches and semi-politicians who wanted a piece-of-cake job running a quiet school in the shadow of the Pines. For the first 15 years of existence, the school was growing too rapidly to really see what was happening. The initial staff members were friends of the local leaders and settled into the school just too comfortably. The school represented a wide rift of different students from wide-ranging economic and social backgrounds. The "antiquated" administration wasn't up to taking advantage of a new school culture that could have raised the status of the school.

There had been some changes at the Board of Education with some people who wanted to see the school seriously upgraded to face the pending new millennium. To the concern of the (growing soft) staff, a new Superintendent was brought in and he fired the entire high school administration.

That's when Matthews entered the scene. The bright and sophisticated black guy from the "city"! He captured the interest of the board with his suave approach, brought in a new administrative team, and began to wreak havoc with the stale teaching staff. He had only been at the school for three years when he hired BJ.

BJ truly believed that this was going to be a new road and a path for him moving forward.

Chapter 11
Visit to Black Pieter –
Wednesday, 28 December 1999

BJ pondered his next steps. The next day he went to the county library to do some additional research into the Pine Barrens. He began to find a number of articles written about the early inhabitants of the region. Stories ranged from the early Lenape presence through the revolutionary influence he had just read to early Stories about run-a-way slaves and tales of Haitian influence pervaded the literature. A resident of the area authored many of these articles: Dr. Peter Santes. BJ googled his name and came up with a rather comprehensive reference on Wikipedia.

His photograph portrayed a very dapper light skinned black man dressed in the usual professorial attire: Jacket with sleeve patches, with a V-neck sweater displaying a colorful tie. He had a bright smile and sparkling eyes. It was difficult to distinguish his age, but based on the copy write date on several of his works, Gleeson guessed him to be in his late sixties.

Santes had his doctorate in Caribbean History. He had taught at Rutgers University at the New Brunswick campus, but had retired and was now doing some adjunct work at Glasgow State College. He preferred to live in a rather rustic cabin somewhere toward the heart of the Pine Barrens.

BJ was surprised to find him in the directory and further surprised when the author-professor, himself, answered his call in a rich a melodious voice. Professor Santes (Please call me Peter!) was most gracious. Initially, the Professor seemed rather skeptical about BJ. He expressed, openly, his concern over his planned "investigation". But BJ provided him with a sound overview of his own research and a short version of the disappearance of Kelly.

The Professor's skepticism turned to an expression of high interest level. He proceeded to invite BJ to visit with him the next day. He warned BJ about the use of GPS in the Pines and gave him some better landmarks to follow. "You don't want to get lost in these woods," he mused jokingly.

Early that Thursday morning, BJ headed down Route 9, swung west on Route 550 and struck out for the middle of Belleplain State Park. The Professor's directions took him just off Route 550 toward the edge of the state park. As he drove, BJ thought about the varied peoples who had inhabited these pines over the past 200 plus years. The "daily hyped" Millennial was just a few days away amidst rumors of catastrophes and fear… How much simpler or perhaps—even more difficult was life for the people who navigated this region in generations past?

As he pulled off Route 550, he entered a heavily forested area that initially looked totally unoccupied. BJ pulled to the side and took out the notes that the Professor had given to him over the phone. As he weaved his way through the road, he began to see signs of rough-hewn homes scattered throughout the pines. These were no mansions, but bordered on the quaint.

They were mostly well kept and attended to. BJ's knowledge of history took him back to the rough-hewn slave cabins that occupied much of the south, from the Carolina's north. He had visited a former Rice Plantation in South Carolina to find that cabins like this were still occupied by small remnants and descendants of the original slaves of the early and mid-1800s. He saw very little evidence of life as he moved deeper in these Pines.

Finally, after what seemed an eternity of following that solitary road and landmarks, he entered a marked dirt road that took him just a few hundred yards to the cabin that Professor Santes had described. It was a neatly kept reasonably new "log cabin" that one can have constructed these days. It appeared to resemble the earlier homes he had passed, but much newer. He was surprised at the sight that he saw on the front porch.

Instead of his concept of a proper professor, sat an older man calmly carving what appeared to be a duck on the front porch. He sat in a rocking chair with a rough-hewn poncho covering his top. As he climbed out of his car, BJ heard the man welcome him.

"Professor Gleeson, so glad you could visit my humble abode." Santes stood up from his chair, he was an impressive 6'6", and BJ hadn't anticipated his size. He offered BJ some lemonade and cookies and gestured for him to sit next to him and a small table in another rocker.

They sat on the porch as BJ quickly began to explain the story of Annie and Kelly and to raise his own questions about what appeared to be the mystery of this area. He asked the professor to shed any of his own research and light in what might be some sort of ritualistic murder.

After his rather brief explanation, Peter leaned back and began to speak about himself and this region where he resided.

"I was raised in North Jersey, but discovered this place during my doctoral research on the Pine Barrens. It was a great place for quiet research and I fell in love with the cabin and its rather secluded location. A lot more private than Newark!

"Once I started college, I found a world outside of the urban city. As I traveled during my studies, I decided to relocate permanently here in the late 1980s. My studies became my life, so I am a rather solitary old man with no family to carry on after me. There are interesting enclaves of small groups living throughout the Pines. I have come to know many of the people. They live near small towns, attend churches, and engage in a variety of rather quaint older customs."

The Professor continued: "Although I still, initially lived in New Brunswick, the more I came down to my cabin, the more the locals seemed to accept my presence and, in many ways, take me into their confidence."

He continued, unabashedly (he certainly liked to talk!):

"There are pockets black people living among the Pines," he continued, "albeit they are still kept rather private and removed. You probably have heard of the 'Jackson Whites' from Northern New Jersey. They are thought to be a mixture of runaway slaves and hessian soldiers from the revolutionary war period. They were (too) frequently Albino with light brown skin and clear blue eyes.

"Generally thought to be from inter-breeding. Until the 1970s, they actually avoided the schools. And game wardens, in that area, had learned, the hard way, not to go up into the hills to check for hunting licenses. The Jackson Whites are the northern versions of hillbillies. Some of them began to settle here toward the end of the Revolutionary War.

"They quickly became a part of the 'patch-quilt' fabric of the Pine Barrens. But since the Pineys have ended up being a very 'blended' population, they have incorporated a wide variety of legends from all countries and ethnicities. One such is an anti-Santa Clause figure from the Germanic regions of Europe.

"As St. Nicholas paraded through the villages of Europe—distributing gifts to the children along the side of the street, he was preceded by a sinister, dark figure known as 'Black Pieter'. Black Pieter carried a quiver loaded with switches. He sought out children who had been 'bad' and whipped them with the switches, while St. Nicholas passed them by with gifts. Children feared Black Pieter, who by the way, is called 'Belsnickel' in many of the Pennsylvania Dutch areas.

"When I moved back to this area, the locals from this area dubbed me with the nickname 'Black Pieter'. I felt it was reasonably interesting but—so I haven't bothered to correct my new neighbors. You probably noticed the scattered cabins as you drove in to find me: these are reflections of that past population that helped to work the fields and farms of this 'Garden State'.

"It may also be that the 'residents' also see me as another 'denizen' of these woods: In the 1800s, there was a black medical doctor, James Still, in these regions who was not allowed to practice because of his race. Some say he was lynched, others said he died of a heart attack. Many in this region still believe he is a patron saint to the Piney community and comes to the aid of injured and stranded travelers in this region. Lost travelers have told stories of a kindly gentlemen who came to their aid when they were lost or hurt in these woods.

"From any perspective, however, I am treated as a very special 'character' by many of my neighbors. I find it quite interesting given my background and training. Rather humorous, since I am a history professor with a Doctorate, but I have to say, I am enjoying this semi-retirement. I go up to Glassboro and teach one or two courses a semester, but I am developing some good friendships in this area—and continuing to learn about the traditions and customs."

BJ identified with the professor. A part of him longed for this sort of rural experience. He got so caught up with these strange tales that he almost forgot that he had come to inquire about Annie, Kelly, and those strange tattoos.

"Peter," he began, "I have encountered an old prostitute from this area who apparently has lost her daughter to some sort of crime. Did you ever hear of Pine-Bog Annie?"

Peter scratched his head, hesitated, and responded, "Everyone in this area knows about Pine-Bog Annie, I've heard that she has been plying her trade on the main roads for well over 20-30 years. Her shack is about a mile-away, on the other side of Lake Mummy. But I have never met the woman—and I don't think I knew that she had a daughter."

BJ continued, "I saw what appeared to be the remains of her daughter. She had two tattoos that appeared rather recent on her arm and chest. Three circles, blue, green, and red, with a rough brown cross in the center. Does this relate to any historical customs or traditions that you know of?"

Peter leaned back in his chair, tilted his head back slightly, and seemed to be deep in thought before he spoke, "You know, that among the slaves in this area were many from the Caribbean islands—some Haitians who brought a mix of Christianity and Pagan beliefs. Along with the story of the 'Jersey Devil' are stories, originating from these Haitians, that focus on the concept of the 'undead' and the belief in a King of the Zombies who returns periodically. I believe I have seen something similar to what you describe used in their rituals.

"I am very interested in working with you to solve this mystery, if you will allow me," proffered Peter. "Feel free to come back and visit. And I do thank you for listening to me ramble on about these Pines that I have come to love!" He handed BJ a rather colorful card with a phone number.

As BJ worked his way back out of the woods, it dawned on him that Peter had never invited him inside his house. But then again, it was a beautiful day and he seemed to enjoy his porch. The inquisitive part of BJ wanted to see how a learned professor actually "lived" in that cabin.

BJ pulled back on the main road and headed for the tavern to fill Jade in on his progress—or lack of it! He was intrigued by 'Black Pieter' and believed that his insights with the area might prove helpful as he refined his newly found "investigative skills". But there were only a few days left in his vacation—and he would be back at the grind, teaching by next week—same time.

The bulky car phone began to flash and squawk and he picked it up as he drove. It was Cassie, reminding him to follow up with his promise to follow up with his own kids. He needed a new life right now. He wasn't quite ready for reunions. But he realized that he needed to reach out, particularly to Carly who was just a stone's throw away in Delaware. He would take care of that soon—he promised himself. It buzzed again! This time it was Jade calling from Staley's.

"How did you make out? Annie is still hanging out here—she is pretty badly broken up—but, at least for now, not drinking."

"I'm coming down to the tavern now and I will fill you in," he replied.

They settled into a corner table once he got back. "Not much for now, but there are some stories about some possible mystical cults that have operated in the region. Not much we can do for Annie unless we get some better and more complete information."

BJ reflected on his progress or lack of same as he drove back home. The police were just not interested in the rather decomposed remains of a hooker lying in a back-woods morgue. It just wasn't on their radar, even though BJ was trying to get them involved. But the Professor seemed to be a valuable asset as he moved deeper into what was now "his" investigation.

Chapter 12
Atlantic City – 31 December 1999

The turn of the century was rapidly approaching, but Gleeson was at one of the lowest points in his life. His girlfriend, Jade, was preoccupied with her work at the bar on what promised to be a very busy weekend. His ex was pissed at him for blowing off Christmas. His kids were distanced from him—both emotionally and by miles.

Again, he found himself on the shore: this time, at Strathmere Beach again, on the Northern portion of Sea Isle City. This time of the year, large empty conch shells washed up on this wide, ignored, potion of the shore. Even though it was cold, he kicked off his shoes and removed his sox. He walked down toward the surf reflecting on the odd collection of shells that were washing up.

He wondered what God had in store for him. He was still a believer, but not practicing very hard at it since his divorce. Again he felt close to God with the power of the waves. He thought about this old lady, herself so broken, wrestling with the loss of a child. He couldn't even come close to contemplating her pain!

He felt like a man between two worlds and wanted to fill that void with something. Maybe he could help to heal Annie's pain by helping her to get some resolution to Kelly's death. *But I'm no detective*, he thought. *I am a good historian, and a decent investigator*. Right there, on that beach, he determined to do all in his power to shed light on Kelly's death. Was it a murder? Was it some cult accident? What did those tattoos mean?

He would be heading back to classes on the following Wednesday and was on his own for the "Millennium", and he could head back to his apartment to do some more research on his computer. But then he decided that upon his return to school on Wednesday he would begin to nose around to find out who knew anything about Kelly. To get a head start he decided to go to his office at school and make some notes to us. In addition, he thought that he might still catch Matthews in his office.

It was after 4 PM As BJ pulled into the school lot, and, as he hoped for, he saw Matthew's bright red new BMW sitting in the "Principal" space. *Good, thought BJ, I can catch him for a few minutes.* He parked his van and walked down the empty school corridor toward the Principal's office. Secretaries had the week off and the main office was empty.

BJ knocked on the door and Mathews happily waved him in. Matthews was in good humor. He had a glass with golden liquid sitting on his desk. "It's after hours, can I pour you one?"

"What is it?" asked BJ.

"It's a top shelf tequila that I brought back from my last trip to the Islands—the best stuff…"

"Sure," said BJ as he sat back with a pour of the special liquid.

"What brings you in here today?" said Matthews.

BJ began to spin the tale of Annie and Kelly and finally asked Matthews, "Did you know anything about that young girl?"

"I don't think I remember her, it was a few years ago, I had just gotten here, but I can walk down to guidance with you to pull her records. By the way, when did you become a detective, I've been grooming you to be an educational leader—not Sherlock Holmes."

"It's just something I am following up on behalf of Jade and Annie," said BJ.

But Matthews continued, "This damn school is just too big, how can anyone really know all 4,000 plus students? Come with me (as he downed his tequila) and we'll check out her records."

BJ downed his drink and they both walked to the empty guidance office. Matthews opened up the master guidance computer and file cabinet. "Nothing particularly special here, shows she was a decent student with a poor attendance record, up until the time she dropped out. Fairly nondescript if you ask me."

"Well, thanks anyway, Clarke, I'll be on my way now." He turned and began to walk toward the parking lot. "Hang on, BJ," Matthews interrupted. "We are having a private get-together at Harrah's on New Year's Eve. I will have one of my other guys give you a call with the details. We would love to have you join us—and (eventually) the team."

BJ felt pretty good as he headed back toward the shore area. Matthews seemed to be warming up to him, even giving him, reluctantly, some help on his "special project".

As it turned out, he got a call from one of his teacher friends—"Crab". Matthews had told him to invite BJ. Some of the single guys were going to make a night of the Millennium with an outing at Harrah's at AC. *What the hell*, BJ thought, *might as well bring in the new millennium by making friends with some new buddies. The school and my new 'investigative' project can be put on hold for the rest of the century.*

It was now late Saturday afternoon as Gleeson moved North on the Parkway toward AC. He reflected on his life as he turned onto the AC Expressway and headed into the city. It felt odd being alone on a New Year's Eve. He would have like to have spent it near Jade, but he thought it was too soon to dive to deeply into a new relationship. In any respect, she was still too heavily involved in the restaurant—particularly on this New Year's Eve.

He pulled into the parking lot and went to the main Casino floor to find his friends. The first person he spotted was his Principal, Clarke Matthews. He was sitting at a wide rectangular bar that was adjacent to the high roller crap table. There were a number of obviously unattached women (probably of the night) stationed at various points of the bar. Matthews was clearly reviewing the available merchandise. He was divorced with two young children, and rumor had it that he roamed far and wide in search of some different tastes. As BJ closed in on him, he decided that the rumors were correct.

Just as he said his first hello to his principal, he heard the voice of his friend Crab who was sauntering toward the bar with two other teachers from the school. BJ didn't really know them, but he knew "Crab" for years before they both reconnected at Pineland Regional. They had spent time working under Matthews at his last school. Crab seemed to be a part of Clarke's inner circle, even though he was not an administrator.

"BJJJJJJJJJJ!" he shouted across the floor. Principal Matthews caught sight of all of them at the same time. Matthews bought a round of drinks for the small crew. He was socially very comfortable, even though he was out drinking mostly with his subordinates. BJ only knew the other two teachers through student reputation, which can be quite accurate.

Casey Kiner was a quiet, tall, and lanky Math Teacher-seemingly well respected by teachers and students. The third man was Will Hoover. He was a smaller, very well dressed man with some rather effeminate affectations. The kids in school said that the "Hoover Sucked". But BJ thought this might just be a good joke with an odd name. As he watched Will move, however, he began to think the students might have had something there.

The last of the crew was one of the three current Vice-Principals. "Doc" Martin was a leftover from the last administrative team. He was pushing retirement but was able to behave like a chameleon with any administrative or teacher group. He was mostly bald with a fringe of white hair around the edges.

He had never been married, but appeared to play the field quite adeptly. BJ wondered if he had any sound educational beliefs to offset his obvious lack of moral fiber. BJ stopped his thinking right there! Who was he to make these sorts of judgments? He needs to just kick back and enjoy ringing in the New Year!

Hoover, Martin, and Matthews moved to the high roller table and found active seats at the action. Casey, Crab, and BJ just sat at the bar as spectators. Martin and the principal occupied seats next to a 60ish guy with a ring of curly silver, hair around a growing bald pate in the front. He stood head and shoulders above the other players at the table.

The game is progressing as the clock continues to click toward midnight. The two educators and the tall greying man are continually raising the stakes. Crab calls the attention of BJ and Casey to the quiet actions of Matthews and his men. Both of them have quietly spoken to the pit boss that brought a 'suit' over from another portion of the Casino.

"They are probably regulars here and need to get their credit raised for the stakes here tonight. It looks like they are both loosing big!" Crab continued quietly to BJ. "I think this is a serious ongoing problem for Matthews. I've been around him in AC enough to know he appears to be getting in over his head."

But as much as they seemed to be losing, the tall older man seemed to be cashing in big time. He and his fellow players near him both gave the appearance of truckers—by virtue of their rough looking attire for New Year's Eve—much less the Millennium. BJ heard the others calling him Big Mac and it called up an alert in his mind to the discussions and stories of the past week. Wasn't that the name of Annie's boyfriend—and Kelly's dad?

Everything paused as the clock neared twelve. Gambling ceased five minutes before. The revelers were loud, but everyone seemed poised for the descent of the new century. Much ado had been made over the past several years: this would be the end of the world; there would be a worldwide technological failure. The casinos all had emergency plans ready in the event of any potential disaster. Temporary battery charged streetlights had been put along the boardwalk. Extra police were scattered throughout the area.

Everything came to a standstill as the clock moved toward mid-night. Both winners and losers stood quietly as the loudspeaker counted down the final minute. Atlantic City 'exploded' with fireworks and noise to welcome in the new millennial. Music blared as people high fived, hugged, while the woman working the room were doling out free hugs and kisses to the men who were standing around. The music began to abate and the gamblers settled in again.

During the pause, Hoover, Martin, and Mathews came back to BJ and his friends at the bar. They both seemed dejected and depressed. They didn't, however, offer any sense of how much they had lost! Big Mac had hit it big. He had cashed in and sat across from BJ's crew on the far side of the bar. Mac was splurging for all of his friends. None of the truckers were feeling any pain. BJ looked at the older man intently. (Could this REALLY be Kelly's father?)

Gleeson nursed his drink so he could watch the show that was developing across the bar. The more they drank, the louder they became. There are happy drunks, crying drunks, and angry drunks. Some drunks run the gamut of all three. BJ waxed philosophically as he looked into the glass of Irish whiskey that he was nursing and watched the floor action at the casino.

His memory took him back to a day when his father took him to Yankee stadium with two of his dad's brothers. His father had two brothers and they all liked to lift a glass together. The problem was that his dad was a "crier", one brother a "laugher", and one brother a "terror". On the way back from the Bronx, a rather heated discussion started in the car—over something BJ didn't even remember.

When they got to the drop-off point at one brother's home in Bergenfield, it boiled over a discussion of their respective wives. As a matter of fact, it was in front of them. One uncle took his wedding ring, tossed it into the weeds, and decided to walk home without benefit of the car. The second uncle began to laugh. The first uncle turned around and threated to beat the crap over the "laugher" and BJ's dad dissolved into tears! Was BJ a combination of all of these men?

His thoughts were jarred back to reality, though, as he watched the reality that was transpiring in front of him. It had indeed been Big Mac's luck that night. He was happily taking care of the entire bar, including the hookers looking to connect with his money. He got mad at some of his friends, but then moved into a maudlin, crying stage. He spoke loudly about an old lover named Pine-Bog Annie. (That grabbed BJ's attention!) He remarks that he might have gotten her pregnant years ago. Then he lamented that he met a beautiful young whore several months ago—who he thought he recognized.

As he waxes on about his love life, some of his drunken buddies start with some crude remarks and the next thing BJ noticed was the out-break of a brutal fight across the bar. AC police are brought in to quell the disturbance and BJ watches carefully as they handcuff Big Mac. As he is led away, BJ hears him sadly lamenting, "I think I fucked my own daughter—I might have killed her."

BJ just stands there and thinks about what he has been watching. By now, it was close to 3:00 AM and the fight had stilled the morning festivities.

BJ brought the news back to Jade at Staley's the next morning. The place was a mess due to the late night party at Staley's. Jade had to sleep on a cot in the back, and then get up early to clean. Surprisingly, Annie was there with her—helping. It seemed that Jade had employed Annie to keep her close, and to keep her 'clean'. It appeared to be healthy for Annie.

BJ pulled Jade aside and they went into the back office—out of Annie's earshot. BJ explained what he had seen that last evening. Had the death been resolved? Was Big Mac responsible for the death of his daughter? Since it was still a holiday Sunday, Jade suggested that Gleeson go back to the AC jail and try to look into the situation.

"Happy New Year," she said, as she reached up to kiss him on the cheek.

He returned the kiss, but to her lips and said: "I'll stop back and fill you in."

An hour or so later, BJ found himself in the Atlantic County Jail where Big Mac had been taken. He name-dropped the friendly contact he now had developed with the State Police and handed the desk Sergeant a card that the officer had given him. BJ spoke of his interest in the disappearance of a friend's daughter that might be connected to the silver-haired drunk in the cell.

Without handcuffs or restraints, Big Mac was brought into a waiting room to meet BJ. He had obviously not been charged with any crimes at this point—other than drunk and disorderly. BJ filled Mac in on his knowledge of Annie and Kelly. He proceeded to describe the bizarre string of events that have brought them together. The big man's eyes welled with tears as he described an encounter late last September. He spoke of "trolling" in Atlantic City in late September and encountering a strikingly handsome and well-dressed young woman. He thought he might have recognized her, but proceeded to engage her services for the evening.

Mac was a good listener and the young woman began to speak about her life in the Pines. Suddenly, Mac became equally repulsed and amazed. Annie had disappeared, at least from his vision, in the early 80s—around the time that this kid was probably born. He hinted at a few more questions until she finally revealed her mother's name as "Pine-Bog Annie".

Mac panicked, he quickly dropped her off on the side of a reasonably deserted road and pulled away in his pickup. He vaguely remembered seeing another vehicle pulling up toward her in his rear view mirror. "I never saw her again," Mac commented, "and I worried that some harm might have come to her—since I haven't seen her since. That's why I said what I said at the casino bar—when I was out of it…"

By the time we finished, he was quietly crying and asking for help to find her killer. "I am thankful that you are working with Annie. Give her my best! Here's my number, call me if I can be of any more help to you or Annie." He left, escorted quietly back to his cell. When BJ checked out at the desk, the Sargent let him know that they would be releasing him later today.

BJ had a bit more information, but Big Mac was clearly not a killer! But how could this new knowledge help BJ with his investigation? BJ headed back to the tavern, with a short trip to the shoreline for even more reflection. He had two more days before school resumed on Wednesday. He would get access to some more history and legends, and begin to look for remnants of legends in this new millennium.

Back at the beach, BJ wrestled with the deluge of images, facts, and legends that were bombarding him. He tried to put things together in his mind as he paced along the water's edge. At this point, a small fish was tossed up on the sand from the last wave. It flapped and floundered until BJ bent over and threw it back into the tide, from which he could escape.

As the fish swam away, he thought of a higher power that "saved the fish", but let Kelly be murdered. But as he was God's agent with the fish, perhaps he had a calling with these circumstances he now found himself in. He walked back up to his cab and drove pensively back home. He made another promise to reach out to his own daughter.

Chapter 13
More Bodies – 2 January 2000

It was Monday, 2 January; BJ had two more days before school resumed. He had stopped for breakfast at Staley's that was fairly empty after the busy weekend. He sat and spoke with Jade. He explained to her about his encounter with Annie's "husband"—Big Mac—and the subsequent talk at the jail. BJ was trying to put his facts together and it helped to have Jade there to guide him through his thinking.

"So, the best I can figure, Big Mac may have been the last person to see Kelly alive. None of this is making much sense to me so far…" He continued, "But we need to help this poor woman find peace—she needs to know what happened to Kelly." He stayed through lunch and then wove his way through the shore towns to another place on the empty winter beach.

He paced along the shoreline and reflected, on a new year, possibly a new love, and a curious adventure which beginning to involve him. He thought again about his Cassie, and her expanding career in NYC, and his two kids, coping with college and a new job. Were they ignoring him or was he ignoring them?

After some additional time of reflection, and even some prayers to the God that controlled that powerful sea, he walked back across the hard sand and up onto the boardwalk. He sat on one of the benches that were strategically and economically (people paid to have their name on them) placed. He noticed a newspaper machine alongside the bench. The headline of the Press from Atlantic City almost screamed out at him. "Three Local High School Students SLAIN"!

The article went on the explain that State Troopers discovered the bodies of three young people, badly mauled and further hinted that there might have been some dismembered of the victims. Names were not released in the preliminary article, only the fact that it was two females and one male.

BJ drove immediately to the state barracks to try to meet with his officer who had been assigned to Kelly's case, Todd, with a noticeable limp. BJ gave his name at the desk and waited to meet Collins in person for the first time. A tall young blond man walked out from behind two office doors.

"Are you Gleeson?" he asked as he moved to the counter. "Let's go to a private office in the back."

"Are you a school teacher or an amateur detective, or maybe a little of both?" said Collins.

"I am just trying to wrap my head around the death of Kelly and the recent uncovered murders of several students from my school. All of a sudden, the two events started to come together in my head," BJ replied.

Collins opened a conference door, BJ stepped in and they both sat down.

"In any respect, thanks for seeing me. I know I might be a bit out of my league, but I also think my studies of this region and history could be of some help."

"On the surface, this is highly irregular, but I think you might be able to shed some insight into the case, even though it is really not my own! But life here in the Pines is pretty boring. It just might be interesting to work with a bright guy like you in a "shadow capacity" to see if, together, we might be able to figure these killings out."

"Sounds very interesting to me, Todd," said BJ.

"But we have to keep this highly confidential. I will classify you as an informant because of your inside view of the high school. The materials I provide for you, however, are highly confidential. You know these local folks don't really care about cases like this.

"I came out of a police family, I have a cousin in the FBI and my dad has retired out of Newark, New Jersey's detective division. I had a fairly serious knee injury playing high school football, that kept me from joining the army, but it didn't keep me from making the force down here!"

BJ commenced to fill Collins in on the high school situation. All three young people had been students at Central Pines. Collins jotted down some names and addresses and quietly slipped them, along with some other papers to BJ while they talked. Collins revealed the rather shocking fact that the three students had all been very recently (within the last few days) been tattooed on their arm and chests. In addition, the left-hand ring finger of each of the victims had been cut off. Todd confirmed to BJ that it was the tricolored symbol that had been found on Kelly.

In addition, Todd revealed that the State Police were working with the AC police on the recent expansion of organized crime. One of the newer drug cartels vaguely connected with remnants of the Pablo Escobar crime syndicate. Although Escobar had been killed in 1993, a tribal group from the northern region of Columbia had picked up a major portion of his trade to the North-Eastern United States. That tribal group also had a history of recent human sacrifices in their homeland.

It now seemed that there might be some connection between this group and the recent increase of cocaine in AC. Given the native background from Northern Columbia, this caused BJ to reflect on the historical work he had been doing. He reflected on the influence of varied groups in the Pinelands. He wondered how Kelly could have been connected to this. Was there a drug connection in the high school that resulted in these deaths? If so, who was behind it? Collins hoped that BJ would be able to dig deeper into the current high school culture.

BJ reviewed his next steps with Todd: 1) He had to locate the tattoo parlor and investigate the ink pattern; 2) He needed to investigate whatever drug movement that was going on at the school; 3) He would need to visit the parents of the slain students—even though this was somewhat out of bounds. They shook hands as BJ left the office and pledged to meet, outside of headquarters regularly until they had resolved the current problem.

BJ returned to school on Wednesday. It was a somber day with the news of three student deaths. The kids were not the most popular in the school. They weren't student athletes, honor society, or theatre geeks—they tended to be more on the fringe. Never the less, many students mourned and wore black armbands in their honor. Small memorials to the three quickly grew on the lawn in front of the school.

BJ just tried to keep his ears open and to listen for rumors or clues as the dour winter week continued. He saw Justine briefly in the hall. He pulled her aside: "Have you heard anything about those kids?"

"There's a lot of talk about drugs and some cult activity—I'll see you at Mom's later."

On Friday morning, however, he had a rather cold and curt note in his mailbox to meet with the Principal at the end of the school day. As he moved through his classes, he pondered what Matthews would have to say to him. When 3:30 PM arrived, Gleeson moved down into the waiting area of the main office. The secretary indicated that Matthews had someone in with him already.

It was Will Hoover, the Biology teacher, who had been with Matthews in Atlantic City. Hoover briefly and rather sullenly recognized BJ as he moved out of the office. Matthews came to the door of his office and genuinely welcomed BJ into a seat. "Doc" Martin was there. He sat down in front of him, not behind his desk. "I just wanted to clear the air about our little 'adventure' in Atlantic City on New Year's Eve," said Matthews.

"What's to clear?" said BJ. "It was good fun and a nice way to welcome in the Millennium."

"Well, I thought you may have noticed the men who came over to me during the crap game. We are frequent customers there and they simply replenish our funds when we run low on a night like that."

"So?"

"I just wanted you to keep that confidential, that's all. By the way, you are doing a great job here and I'm looking forward to a great future working with you. Have a great weekend." He stood up, indicating that the meeting was over, so BJ took the hint, shook Martin's hand, and left. Martin hadn't said one word during this brief meeting.

That's interesting, thought BJ, *he has never EVER seen me teach. His knowledge of me was just from the last place and we were never that close then. Why is he taking me so much into his confidence and inner circle?*

As BJ drove back to his apartment, he thought carefully about some of the rumors that floated on both Matthews and Hoover. There is a good bit of talk in the faculty room about Matthews womanizing—particularly with a board member's wife. He has also been seen "checking out the female merchandise" on the AC Board walk. But he was, after all, now single and free to spread his wings—providing it wasn't with someone in the school circle.

He heard more about Hoover from the students. Students think he goes "both ways". They claim that he has been involved—outside of school hours— with some of the fringe students in the school. The students also are aware of the prevalence of drugs, particularly coke, that are available on campus.

BJ made a turn onto route 50 and headed back towards the police barracks. He needed to reconnect with Collins but, then again this wasn't a major FBI investigation, it was a rather informal procedure occupying the time of Pinelands troopers who usually just handled traffic and family disputes. This might be about to change!

When he pulled into the barracks lot, he saw the desk Sergeant walking toward his car. "Sarge," BJ called out.

"Hey BJ, what's up at this time on a Friday?"

"Well, Matt, I just wanted to give you a short update on this week at Pinelands and my interactions with the students, faculty and administration. I hope to wrestle some additional insights over the next week or two. Confidentially, there may be some gambling problems between the AC casino and the Principal his Vice-Principal and another teacher, Will Hoover. I will look into this and get back to you."

On a serious note, Collins warned BJ to be careful but then he looked at Gleeson, almost whimsically, "Well Detective Gleeson—are you having fun yet with this. What you're doing could be very valuable, but don't let this get out of hand."

BJ told Collins that he was going to try to "interview" the parents of the slain students, but Collins gave him a stern warning. BJ explained that he would be doing this simply as a gesture from the school. Reluctantly, Collins just—again—told him to "watch his step". As they parted, BJ smiled and admitted that he was enjoying his research and would continue to share. They both got into their respective cars and headed out for the weekend.

As he drove towards his apartment, and subsequently his beach refuge, he pondered how to go about contacting the three sets of parents. He decided that he would contact each set of parents as a school representative or perhaps pass himself off as the school grief counselor? Since Matthews was still being nice, although somewhat strange, with him; he would let the Principal know that he was doing this in the interest of the entire school—and that he would keep Matthews posted. He hoped Matthews would buy that story for now.

He had secured the addresses and telephones of the parents through guidance. He would wait a week or two until the funerals and burials were complete to make the contacts. In the meantime he began to do an internet search to find out what he could about the three families.

The students were: Ruth Secore – 16-year-old junior; Annette Corbett – 17-year-old junior; and Vincent Dinero – 18-year-old senior. Interestingly enough, two of the parents all had different last names as the result of divorces. He had to dig through their files to secure the appropriate addresses and information.

Ruth's parents resided in a reasonably upscale, new community, just outside of Atlantic City. Her parents both worked at different casinos in Atlantic City. Her stepfather was a floor manager at resorts and her mom was the head of the restaurant service. They were an upscale economic family with plenty to provide for their only child—except time and love!

Annette lived in a similar community, further south. She lived with her widowed mother and two younger brothers who were still in the area middle school. Her mother was, now, independently wealthy after the death of her second husband. He was a top-level executive at Caesar's.

Vincent had come from a very different background. His roots were with an Italian family in a reasonably secluded area of the Pine Barrens. He had two older brothers who were already out of high school and working in the building trades.

BJ had some interesting visits to schedule. He hoped that should relieve his pending boredom over the winter. At that point he picked up his cell phone and called his son, James, in Missouri. James answered on the first ring. "Glad to hear from you, Dad, how is life in Sea Isle City?"

"I'm settling in, but I hear from your mother that you are flourishing in the legal world of Missouri. Corporate law—that sounds pretty safe and secure."

"It's going well, but I want to catch up with you. When can you get out here? I'm really tied up on a busy schedule. I'll even fly you out here!"

"I don't know when I will be able to get away, probably not until Easter break or maybe the summer, but thanks for the offer. Great to know your son can spring for a plane ticket. I miss you and hope we can stay in touch better until we can meet. You know I love you, even if I don't show it enough."

"Me too, gotta go, Dad, another client's at my door, talk to you again soon."

It sounded a little to BJ of Harry Chapin's *Cats in the Cradle* song.

BJ was on a roll now, so he took the opportunity to call his daughter as well. The phone rang several times and then went to voice-mail. It pleased him to hear her voice: "Sorry I missed you, Dad, thought we could talk and arrange a time for me to come down and meet you for lunch. Love you, Dad!"

BJ put his phone back down and forced himself mentally to return to the here and now; he just had to carefully make sure that Clarke Matthews is OK with his guidance activities as he moved forward.

Chapter 14
Cult Figures at the Cristiana Mall –
17 January 2000

For the next two weeks in January, BJ juggled a number of balls in the air. His thoughts were still with his kids and (even) his ex-wife. He was becoming increasingly wrestles and bored with his teaching schedule. He was having difficulty motivating his students, even when he digressed to his novel historical episodes! And it wasn't even close to baseball season. He was drawing closer and closer to Jade.

But what truly dominated his thinking was this string of odd deaths in this part of the state riddled with legends and a strange blend of a variety of cultures. All of these seemed to converge in the heart of the Pines—Native Americans, runaway slaves, deserting British soldiers.

Inter-relationships over the last two centuries have resulted in an interesting blend and color in many of the citizens of these regions. Even Jade seemed to have a darker hue than many of her peers in the bar. And she grew up in Bergen County!

What would tie all of this together? Was he just searching to avoid grappling with life? What about Atlantic City, the mob, and the gamblers? Then there was this influx of the native Columbians. He combined all of this with the strange cults that he constantly heard about. Did he have any business in this series of events, or was he just out of his element? But, after-all, he was a dedicated historian – not a private detective. Then again, how does one become a "private detective"? Some were retired cops, but others were just inquisitive individuals with persistent personalities. Why couldn't that be him!

In the middle of all of this was BJ's need to reconnect with his kids and smooth the waters between he and his ex-wife. He had reopened the conversation with James in Missouri. He was calling him now every week. But

Carly was a different story. For the first few times, all he got was voice mail. Finally, in early January, his phone rang and it was Carly! His heart skipped a quick beat as he picked up her call.

"Finally, we connect," responded BJ.

"Dad, I really do miss you, I agree with you—I want to meet you soon," said Carly.

"Mom said you are pursuing a career as a physician's assistant."

"Yes, I found out you don't need a medical degree, yet starting salaries are well above anything we could get in teaching or nursing…I'm looking forward to it. I also start an internship in this area which pays me well enough to maintain my apartment down here in Dover."

BJ responded, "Great, I will call you in a day or so to set up a meeting time. I love you and can't wait to see you." He felt so positive that he had responded to Cassie's requests and reached out to both of his children. He needed to continue this to enhance his future.

He shared a little of this with, Jade who was trying hard to lift him out of the morose and depression that he had been demonstrating. Jade was quiet, at first, but then assured him that he was doing the right thing in reaching out to them. Even an evening at the ocean hadn't been as calming for him.

Martin Luther King day was approaching on Monday, 17 January. Instead of a celebration, the holiday, originally signed into law by President Reagan in 1983, had quickly evolved into another gigantic shopping day. Jade convinced BJ to spend a day at the Mall with her on his day off. He wasn't a shopper but he relished spending a whole day with Jade, away from this mess.

BJ wasn't usually a late sleeper, but that morning he didn't wake until after 8:00 AM! As he clambered out of bed and made his breakfast, he was beginning, again, to dread stepping foot back into that school on Tuesday. Even though Matthews seemed to be highly friendly and supportive, there was an eeriness that invaded him when he saw Matthews and his crew together. He again worried that he was being pulled into that tight circle.

It returned when he saw the "misfit" students gathering in the corners of the hallways. BJ was looking forward for an escape. Even more, anxiously awaiting the drive and a quiet lunch with Jade—away from the Pines. He was not sure where this relationship was going, but right now—in his life—Jade was filling a major gap!

As he pulled into the lot at Staley's, Jade stood smiling waiting for him outside. She appeared to be overdressed for a trip to the Mall. She wore a green silk blouse with two open buttons on the top. This was combined with a beige short skirt, black tights, and high-heeled boots. BJ quietly began to drool on the inside, while trying to look cool and collected on the outside. She was touching something in him that he had not felt in a long while—and it wasn't just her outfit.

The Christiana Mall was just about one hour away in Delaware. That was the favorite stomping grounds for South Jersey-serious shoppers. Great stores, nice restaurants, and low taxes…you can make a great day of it! As he pulled into the Mall parking lot, he thought about possibly meeting his daughter here, or possibly driving the extra hour down to Dover.

Jade and BJ were both escaping. No stories of Annie or Kelly this morning. They were clearly disturbing for Jade. Instead they spoke, tentatively, about their futures. They swapped stories about their respected checkered pasts. He opened up, albeit partially, about his transgressions in his first marriage and about the pain he felt for his grown children's absence in his life. He spoke about his recent attempts to reconnect with both of them. Jade seemed fully supportive of him in this regard.

In exchange, she shared the abuse that her ex-husband, dead for over 7 years, had perpetrated on her and her daughter. They listened intently to one another as they walked through parking lot and into the Mall.

They wandered rather aimlessly around the Mall, stopping into small shops. BJ was looking for some designer jeans for more formal wear. He also wanted a pair of boots. Jade began tried to drag him into Victoria's Secret, but he resisted—yet fantasized about her. (Probably her ploy!) After a few hours and a few dollars spent (he found a nice pair of boots and she had a package from VS) that she teased him with.

They found a nice Italian restaurant with an indoor-outdoor area. They sat, initially with two glasses of Chianti and watched the mall action—particularly the teenagers who seemed to live here when school was not in session. She ordered an antipasto salad while he indulged in a meatball parmesan sandwich.

They had just ordered their second glass of Chianti when Jade called BJ's attention to a small group of kids who had just seemed to enter the Mall. The group was composed of three girls with two guys, all appeared to be of high school age. The girls had a punk, gothic look—with jet-black hair and facial piercings. The guys almost looked like they were in uniform. They were wearing a combination of blue, red, and green. On the back of one guy's jacket was the symbol of the tricolored/ crude cross that BJ had seen on Kelly's body and been identified in the recent student slayings.

Both Jade and BJ shot to attention, but their second glass of Chianti arrived and they ate and drank quietly while they observed the kids actions in the mall center. Their appearances were drawing attention from other shoppers, but they seemed to relish the attention! They threw taunts at any one who stared at them. They began to bully some very average looking kids, who quickly moved away from them.

BJ and Jade couldn't hear them, but it was clear that their words were upsetting people. They then turned their attention to several senior citizens who were sitting in the center area of the Mall. BJ couldn't quite hear, but it seemed that they were obviously throwing barbs and insults. Someone must have alerted the Mall Police and two of them came to talk with the group. After some, apparently heated discussion, they headed, angrily, toward the exit.

"We need to follow them," said BJ, he drained his Chianti, got the check, which he quickly paid in cash, and grabbed Jade by the arm. He rushed her out to his car while they tried to follow the kids. They slowed down their walk but quietly marked the kids as they moved toward their respective cars. BJ was determined to follow them at a safe distance. They had Jersey plates, BJ asked Jade to write down the license number, as they headed back across the Delaware River into South Jersey.

BJ got that eerie feeling back as he found himself retracing their route back to the Pines. After crossing back into New Jersey, the teens took the first major exit for Route 49. Traffic began to thin out and BJ had to drop further back. At several points Jade thought she saw one of the girls looking back at them from the rear seat and pointing at them. They began to speed up. So did BJ! Within fifteen minutes they hit the intersection for Route 347 South, as they exited, the teens floored their gas pedal and BJ lost them as they sped off into the Pines!

He needed to get back to Sergeant Collins. But first he had to drop Jade off at the Tavern. Jade didn't seem very happy with his abrupt end to the day. In spite of this, BJ quickly headed back out to the Trooper Barracks office. Once again, Collins was on his way out while BJ was pulling in.

"You again, don't you ever take a day off?"

"I should say the same about you, Sarge," retorted BJ.

"If you are going to continue to pick my brain, you could at least by me a beer."

BJ and Collins ended up at a nearby chain eatery. PJ's was known for their wings and craft beers all over New Jersey and Pennsylvania. It was a good place to find a corner booth and meet over the din of 40 large screen TVs.

Gleeson handed Collins the license plate number and began to give him an account of the teens they had seen in Cristiana. Collins agreed to try to identify the plates. Both agreed that there seemed to be a direct connection with a number of factors in this developing "case".

The multicolored cross symbol seemed to be the connecting factor. Where was that from? What did it mean? The two men had created an interesting bond over a few meetings. Gleeson was not great at making friends, but he seemed to be connecting with Collins (call me Todd). After the third pint for each, they decided to call it an afternoon—since it was barely 5:00! BJ agreed to do some further research and Todd decided to see what else was available on the license plates, the AC connection, and the growing drug problems in the area.

He called Jade as he headed back to his apartment.

"That was some way to end a day at the Mall!" she retorted.

"I'm sorry, Jade, but I had to get back to Collins to fill him in and to give him the license information you wrote down."

"Well, I guess now you have to wait awhile to see what I bought at Victoria's Secret."

BJ was perplexed: was she still pissed or was she just teasing him? He apologized to her once more and she hinted that he might get to see her purchase soon. As he continued his drive back to his apartment, he reflected on the recent events—particularly on that multicolored cross that seemed to keep appearing, both in historical literature and in the present circumstances. That retired professor just might be able to help.

Maybe Professor Santes could shed some more light on the situation. He seemed to possess a much deeper and richer understanding of the region than BJ ever would have. BJ had to make another appointment. Peter could be a great asset for him as he works on his new (and actually first) case! (BJ was beginning to internalize that he was morphing into an investigator. If that even happens?)

Chapter 15
Valentine's Day – 14 February 2000

Sunday morning, BJ bolted up from a sound sleep. He found that he had sweat through his nightshirt, shorts, and the sheets that covered his bed. Was he falling ill, or was he just succumbing to the pressure of the past two and a half months? He staggered into his shower in order to prepare himself for his visit to a local church service that he had found. He dried himself off, put on slacks, a dress shirt, and a sweater. Put on a small pot of coffee and threw some bread into the toaster.

What was he doing with his life and where was he headed? His life was beginning to spin out of control. Just over two months ago, he had led them to the discovery of Annie's daughter Kelly's body. He since proceeded to uncover several bizarre past historical examples of ritualized murders in the New Jersey Pines that had some similarities to her death. He accomplished this through his persistent research at local libraries and historical societies.

His high school was in a quiet turmoil over the apparent murder of three students. Principal Matthews seemed even stranger after the incident BJ observed in Atlantic City. He found it difficult to concentrate on teaching traditional lessons to students who seemed to be in a constant grieving space.

But as BJ became increasing embroiled in these murders, he also found himself falling slowly in love with Jade. But at the same time, he was reconnecting with his two grown children, and inadvertently, his ex-wife.

Thankfully, however, BJ felt that he had made two new good contacts and friends, in Todd Collins from the State Police and Dr. Peter Santes, the retired history professor. Both were providing valuable help and assistance as he continued his rather amateur adventures!

The calendar seemed to be driving many of these events. The eventful events at Atlantic City on the Millennium seemed to set in motion a string of events that were attached to specific dates. BJ and Jade had their fateful encounter with a strange group of students on Martin Luther King Day.

BJ was planning to put some more plans into action when he had time over President's weekend. And here it is with Valentine's Day tomorrow! Even that date bothered BJ, since St. Valentinus was brutally martyred in 269, and later became Saint Valentine in 496. It was a far cry from the hearts and candy of modern times. It would, however, be a difficult day in the high school where the students were still in a semi-stupor over the death of their classmates.

BJ had arranged for a quiet dinner for he and Jade in a nice restaurant just outside of Atlantic City. They both needed to get away from the tavern and the people that were gravitating to them over the recent events!

Following their trip to the Mall, it seemed to BJ that many of these issues were beginning to come to take shape into some sort of, as yet, un-definable pattern. Two weeks had passed since Jade and he had encountered that group of students at the Mall. Todd Collins had run the license plate number and surprisingly the car that they were driving was registered to William J. Hoover: The strange teacher who was a close friend of Matthews. Todd and BJ decided it would be better for BJ to follow up on that connection.

In addition, BJ planned to sit down with Principal Matthews to try to find out more about the slain students and to get a sense of what, if anything, Matthews had to do with these events and to try to determine Hoover's influence.

Shortly after BJ got out of church, his phone hummed and he was surprised that it was the Professor: "BJ, I've been thinking a lot about your visit and I did read about more bodies that were found. Some of my local friends have been speculating about the events. Perhaps we need to sit down again. I think I may be able to give you some help."

"Professor, thanks so much. I believe that I am seeing a pattern as well. I'll try to get together with you sometime in the next few weeks. In the meantime, see what else your research can reveal to this situation. It almost is beginning to appear to be cult-based."

BJ spent a good portion of Sunday in quiet reflection on all of this. Once school resumed tomorrow, he would have a full plate, what with his lessons, and preparations for his upcoming baseball season. He would be scheduling a meeting with Matthews, setting up interviews with parents of the slain students, and meeting with both Todd Collins and the Professor at different times.

On Sunday afternoon, he reached out to James and Carly, as he had promised. (I'll call them weekly!) Both conversations went well. James was going to look at flying in for a visit sometime near Easter. He would be setting up a visit with Carly in Delaware very soon.

On Monday, BJ made an appointment to see Matthews, taught his classes, and tried to speak with student's who seemed upset and distraught with the events surrounding these recent deaths. Shortly after school was out, BJ drove to Staley's to pick up Jade for an early supper. He had made reservations at the Smithville Inn, just outside of Atlantic City. They sat at the restaurant bar waiting for their table.

They each had a cocktail before they were seated. BJ filled Jade in on all the most recent news and then just relaxed and listened to her talk about the tavern and her daughter Justine. He felt so special in her presence and he suspected she did also. He brought her back to the tavern around nine since she still had to close up. They sat in the parking lot for a while and talked some more—then kissed deeply—before they separated for the evening. *Celebrating Valentine's Day on a Monday actually really sucks*, thought BJ.

As BJ drove home that evening, he realized that the next two or three months could bring an end in sight to some of these mysteries and questions that he was uncovering. But he truly could never predict what was actually about to happen in and with his life!

Chapter 16
President's Weekend –
17–21 February 2000

Events quieted down for the remainder of January through mid-February. South Jersey got hit with an unusual winter storm that dumped some unexpected inches on the entire region. It restricted BJ but the school snow day left him lots of time to continue his historical research and his private detective work in and around the school.

It was the beginning of President's weekend. That meant two days off from school. BJ found himself on the beach again! This remained the only place that he could regularly find peace and comfort. It gave him time to think more about his two children and particularly about Carly.

He still needed to set up a lunch date with her. It had been two weeks since Jade and he had encountered what they had dubbed as the "cult kids" at the Christiana Mall.

BJ was back at the school, paying particularly careful attention to the "at-risk and uninvolved" student population. These were the kids who generally showed more ink and piercings. Could these kids be involved in some drug-related cults? And, by the way, these kids always seemed to be hanging around the teacher, Hoover, during lunch and after school. Why?

He began holding certain students back from class and asking them some general questions like, "Did you know any of those three kids? What were they up to? Have you heard anything about some sort of private club?" All he got, however, were some general answers. He wasn't that "in with the students" to expect a full confessional!

Principal Matthews was acting highly cordial, yet strange towards BJ. Sometimes BJ just felt like the ax was going to fall on his career at Pinelands Regional; or was this just the paranoia of the events that were bothering him.

But, that was BJ; he was a worrisome individual dealing with his own issues of self-worth over what he considered his life failures to this point in his life.

And Matthews still spoke about the promotions that BJ had in the near future (but had never asked for). But something was still bothering him! BJ's saving graces, however, were his classes (he loved history) and his students appeared to be highly engaged. Baseball season was still a few months off and he could really dive deep into his history.

He was also beating himself up over his relationship with Jade. Down deep, BJ was really a shy guy, and was still having trouble, so soon after his own formal divorce. It was, in hindsight, that she was ready for him on their "date" to the Mall, but he blew it with his absorption in the murders and desire to follow the cult kids.

Even though BJ was just 5 years older than Jade, she had been divorced for over 7 years—and had adjusted to life as a single mom, career individual. Running Staley's was more than a full time job. In addition, her daughter, Justine, was pushing 17 and a student at Central Pines. Although drawn to Jade, he was still suffering the scars from his very recent past. This had gotten particularly difficult as a result from the call from his ex and his conversations with his children.

He kicked up sand and picked up a starfish, as he wandered thoughtfully along the edge of the waves. He was literally escaping into this vague and mystical set of murders. He was no detective! What was he doing here? He headed back to his apartment, determined to do some additional digging into what now appeared to be a string of connected killings.

Search engines were fast becoming great sources for gathering information. Bill Gates had just announced his retirement from Microsoft to dedicate his life to charity. Steve Jobs, of Apple fame, was struggling with cancer, which would take his life the next year.

Working on the shoulder of these giants, BJ used a number of word triggers to look into similar murders in the area over the past few years. As he search words like "Cults"; "Pine Barrens"; "Murders"; "South New Jersey"; he began to download articles that might be helpful.

It was 2:30 AM in the morning. BJ sat with a pile of downloaded articles, too many to be carefully reviewed this night. He started to fall asleep in his bed without even taking off his clothes, when his phone hummed. It was late but he looked at the number. "Oh brother, it's her again!" he thought.

"BJ, sorry to call you so late."

Well, this is a different tone? What's going on here? he mused as he answered.

"That's OK. I was just going down for the night, what's up?"

"I have been talking to the kids and I guess you seriously took my advice—they are grateful that you reached out to them, particularly Carly."

"Well, you DID make the point, even though the hammer was fairly blunt! I am becoming clearly aware of my shortcomings. I think my recent experiences have sharpened my sensitivities for others."

"What experiences are you talking about?"

BJ briefly outlined the work that he was doing on behalf of Pine-Bog Annie.

"Carly indicated that you were involved with some type of informal investigation. I hope you can stay out of trouble. Look, I'll let you get your sleep; I just wanted you to know that I appreciated what you are doing with our children. Goodnight BJ." Cassie hung up.

BJ sat on the edge of the bed with the telephone still in his hand. Cassie moved from "Benjamin" to "BJ"—that was interesting. Maybe he was getting on a better path in all directions. His head hit the pillow and he instantly zonked out for a peaceful rest.

It was Saturday morning, BJ got up and drove to Staley's to have breakfast with Jade. He needed a fresh approach for the rest of his work. He was surprised to see Annie in the kitchen, looking sober and refreshed. Jade and BJ went to their corner table so that BJ could share his latest news.

"I found lots of articles, some references to murders, all of the last 15 or so years. I want to go back to my apartment and try to sort through all the stuff I downloaded. Maybe we can get together after you close tonight?"

"Sounds great, maybe you drive down to my home, Justine (her daughter) will be going out with some friends and you can bring up a bottle of wine for us to share."

After several coffees, a pile of corned beef hash, and pancakes, BJ headed back to his apartment in Sea Isle City for his weekend research. BJ always liked puzzles and these articles looked like an interesting one.

He spread his papers out on his bare living room floor and tried to sort the articles by date. By the time he was finished, he was surprised to fine only about three piles of articles emerged. One included articles from early '86. The second group had articles from early '93, and the latest batch September through January 1999-2000. He began to organize and review each of the three batches.

His first "sort" was from the 1986 series of articles. He had found that most of his sources had come from the Express of Atlantic City, the Daily Journal of Vineland and the Cape May County Herald. There were occasional articles of small coverage from the Star Ledger out of Newark and the Record, out of Bergen County. These papers had a reasonable circulation in South Jersey due to the shore traffic and homeowners who had relocated.

None of the articles he had culled were headline grabbers; most were buried on the lower bottom of a page or in the rear.

His first hit was related to two main headlines: The Bears had just defeated the Patriots to win Super Bowl 20, played in New Orleans. Two days later, the space shuttle Challenger disaster occurred. This was page one on all the papers. Reasonably hidden on page 1 on 26 January was a report of 5 teenagers who had gone missing after attending a rock concert held at the Resorts International Casino. They were all from Cape May city and had driven to the casino in one car. The articles stopped shortly after that.

Under the Challenger article, two days later, was a report on the five teens. Their car had been found deserted at a Parkway Rest-stop just outside of Sea Isle City. Police had an all-points bulletin out for the youth.

Several days later, some of the local papers reported finding one of the boys from the group, dead and mutilated in a point further south off the Parkway. No mention of other bodies. BJ reflected back on the year, the explosion in space, and the passionate and tender response of President Reagan.

But this was also the year he was washing out of baseball, listening to the tunes of Madonna and Whitney Houston. On top of that, a young heavyweight boxer named Mike Tyson was appearing on the scene that February. And in the middle of all that history, five teenagers disappear in the Pines with hardly a blip on the screen!

The second batch of articles was all from 1993. This time the Super Bowl jumped to the front page on 17 January as the Dallas Cowboys defeated the Buffalo Bills by a score of 30-20 in California. Three days later, 20 January, newly elected president, William Jefferson Clinton was sworn in, and on 3

February, the headlines were filled with the pending trial over the beating of Rodney King.

As BJ continued his search, buried under these three headlines was another partial story of mayhem: 3 young girls, ages 15-17 disappeared after a Sweet Sixteen party held on Saturday, 18 January at the Sweetwater Casino, a beautiful restaurant and catering house (not a gambling facility) on the banks of the quiet Mullica River—at the edge of the Pine Barrens. A father picking up the three girls couldn't find them when he came back to the Sweetwater at the end of the event.

The next article was a week or so later, with the Rodney King event on the main headline. This time was a reference to the discovery of an unidentified and badly mutilated young woman found washed up on the shore of the nearby river.

BJ found it surprising that there seemed to be very little additional attention paid to any of these incidents. He attributed this to the coincidence of "big news" which drove these stories to the sidelines. He made a note to check on police reports with Todd Collins.

By now, it was past 9:00 PM. Jade would be expecting him. He jumped out on Route 9 and headed south toward Jade's home in the Belleplain. He got within a mile and realized he forgot the wine. He jammed on the brakes and turned off into a liquor store just on the corner.

He picked a bottle of red and a pint of Irish whiskey, tossed down some cash, and headed back out. Jade's place was sequestered deep in the forest. There were other nice homes along the street leading into her house. As he pulled into the driveway, he saw three large dogs bounding toward the car.

Justine was still there and called them all in. Justine was preparing for a sleepover with one of her girlfriends. BJ imagined that this was Jade at 16! Tall and tan, and young and lovely, another girl from Ipanema… She said hello to BJ, grabbed an overnight bag, and kissed her mother, saying, "You two lovebirds, behave!"

It also struck BJ that Justine was a student in his school and he hardly ever saw her! This could be another avenue to more seriously pursue as he studied the student population.

Jade turned to BJ as Justine left the apartment. "You've had too much on your mind, let me open up your bottles and pour for both of us." She came back with her wine glass and a jigger of Irish whiskey neat—the way she knew he liked it. They kicked back on her couch; Jade had gotten the fireplace roaring. She spread out the notes that BJ had handed to her.

BJ began, "I've really been ignoring you big-time over the last few weeks. This situation with Annie really has gotten to me. I might be well over my head and outside of my abilities."

"Don't get down on yourself, your heart is in the right place…even if your head isn't!"

BJ continued, "I don't know where WE are just now? I'm drawing closer to you, but a part of my is afraid to go deeper into a new relationship."

"I've been alone for the past 15 years so you have some time to get used to me."

BJ downed his Irish whiskey too quickly. He paused and began to fill Jade in on his research. "Where were we both 15 years ago? I was the middle of what I thought would be a great baseball career and you were in the process of divorce. And neither of us knew anything about each other."

Jade was just casually listening to him, sipping her wine slowly, and perusing his summary of the articles. Suddenly she stopped and raised her head toward BJ. "Take a close look at the years from these articles, BJ, 1986, 1993, and now it's 2000! It seems that these murders occur every seven years around the same time! Young people, Pine Barrens, brutal murders… What—if any— is the connection? What, if anything, does numerology have to do with these hideous events?"

BJ showed astonishment. "How did I miss that? I thought it was rather odd that the dates were separated. All of this from Cape May to Atlantic City!" He began to piece together all that he had read: the wild tales from the Pine Barrens, the Rise of the Mob that came with the Casino Industry, the "Cult Kids at the Mall", and the possibility of infiltration of the mob by the Columbians. He thought of the stories that Peter Santes had spun for him as they sat on the porch of his house in the Pines.

He and Jade talked into the night, but their history journey began to fade as Jade finished her bottle of wine, while he emptied his pint! They soon were inter-twined on the couch. The next thing BJ remembered were both of them waking up early in the morning in her bed—sans clothes and with warm thoughts of what had transpired.

Chapter 17
The Interviews – 21 February 2000

He got up quietly, dressed, and headed back to his own place. He could still smell the fragrant scent of the warm fireplace on his sweater. As he drove, he began to plan for his visits to these parents, now that the immediate grief had slightly subsided. He decided he would do the two girls' (Ruth and Annette) parents first and finish off with the boy's (Vincent) family since they were much further inland. He would try reaching them on Sunday and, possibly meeting with them on Monday since school was not in session for President's Weekend. (For that's what Washington's birthday had become!)

He prepared the same "script" as that he would use when making the telephone calls: "Hello, this is Mr. Gleeson calling on behalf of Pinelands Regional. Our Principal, Dr. Clarke Matthews, has asked me to reach out to you. The school is planning a memorial, and I have been asked to meet with the parents to decide on the most sensitive and best way to remember the students. I promise not to take too much of your time during this most difficult period."

On Sunday, surprisingly, he reached both of the mothers within the hour. He had more difficulty catching up with the Dineros but he reached that family later in the evening. He could tell from their voices that they were all still struggling, but they all appeared to welcome his visit and he scheduled all three visits on the following day. He would be able to make the two upscale homes in the morning, grab lunch, and head down to the Pines for the afternoon visit. Ruth's home was located in Somer's Point, Annette's was in Seaville, and Vincent was inland in Tuckahoe.

He headed North on Route 9 to the Somer's Point address. It was easily located in a fairly new development. It was a nice sized colonial, set back from the road. He pulled into the driveway around 9:30 and made his way to the front door. A very handsome, well-dressed woman greeted him at the door. A taller man stood directly behind her. "I am Jennifer Johnson and this is my husband Randy, I am Ruth's mother, you must be Mr. Gleeson, please come in. My husband and I took the morning off to meet with you."

"Thank you, Mr. and Mrs. Johnson, I can only imagine how difficult the past few weeks have been, but thank you for having me. As I noted, we are planning some type of memorial at the school and thought you could offer some thoughts about Ruth that would help with our planning."

"Ruth was so looking forward to college planning," offered Mrs. Johnson. Mr. Johnson just sat quietly alongside her on the sofa, placing his hand on her shoulder and leg intermittently. "She really didn't have a lot of friends in that school so I am a bit surprised at the memorial concept. She wasn't a cheerleader or an athlete; she wasn't in the band, chorus, or theatre club. She just went about her business with her small group of friends."

"I gather that she was fairly close with Annette and Vincent?" offered BJ.

"She was very close with Annette, they were best friends, but I didn't know Vincent that well. I really don't know how he ended up with them."

"You know, the police went through a lot of this with us. What is your point?" interjected Mr. Johnson with some frustration. "I'm really not sure what you are looking for here. You need to leave my wife alone, she has been through enough."

"Sorry, but we at the school are equally disturbed to see this having occurred with our three students, and like you, we would like to see some resolution. We really believe we can help!"

"I think we're done here!" said Mr. Johnson. He stood and moved toward the area of the door. He was obviously upset by BJ's presence.

"I'm sorry if I disturbed you but if you have anything else you would like to share, please contact me at the school." Mr. Johnson said nothing as he slowly but firmly closed the door behind BJ.

BJ was feeling rather dejected. He thought he had not gotten off to a good start on the interview scene. But, maybe this wasn't such a great idea after all. He got in his van and headed back down Route 9 towards Annette's house in Seaville. He needed a better approach at his next stop. He thought through some new strategies to use in that home.

Thirty minutes later he found himself outside of what could only be called a small mansion. A large home was planted far back on a beautiful tree framed property. This was no development but there were other similar homes on large properties in the area.

Mrs. Gail Corbett answered to door. She had dark rings under her eyes and signs of ongoing tears and crying. Nevertheless, she welcomed BJ into her living room. He decided to use the different approach with her.

"How can we help?" he began. "Is there anything we can do, from the school's perspective, to assist you and your boys?"

"Thanks, but I don't know what's next. I lost my husband to a sudden heart attack last year, and now this! I am doing everything I can to keep it together for my boys. They are in middle school right now—and that's a difficult enough stage…"

"Is there anything you can tell me about Annette, that might allow me to help. I am trying to help people sort this horror out. I have a good friend who just lost her daughter. I think there might be some sort of a pattern." BJ thought he had a good listener here who might be willing to share.

"How well did she know Ruth and Vincent?"

"Know…that's interesting, I even shared this with the police, Annette and Ruth were very close friends. They were even planning to go to the same college. But this guy, Vincent, seemed to show up out of the blue and into their lives. I couldn't figure it out, he was a nice enough guy, but you know, a little strange. I think he lived in the Pine Barrens, even though he's not what I would call a 'Piney'."

"I heard that the three of them all got the same tattoo. Did she tell you anything about that?"

"Well, she never had a tattoo or spoke of getting one. Her and Ruth were college preppies, if you know what I mean. It was small and she never told me about it. One of my boys saw it though and blew the whistle on her. But I'm now a single mom and the boys were into far more trouble than Annette, so I kinda let it slide by. I suspect it was Vincent's idea."

"Were they spending a lot of time together, was Vincent's somebody's boyfriend?"

"Just friends, you know kids today, they don't 'date' like we used to. They just 'hang out'. I did hear, from the boys again (they are my junior detectives), that they were going to some sort of 'meetings' in the Pines with Vincent."

"I'm sure you shared all this with the police?"

"Actually, the police didn't really seem to be very interested in this. They asked a few questions and left me alone, they didn't even talk to my boys!"

BJ offered, "Would you mind if I spoke to them now?"

She agreed and called the boys down from their room.

BJ introduced himself and they chatted for a bit, about baseball and school, then he began:

"What's about these 'meetings' your sister was going to? Did she ever tell you about them?"

"Well, you know girls!" one brother offered. "They don't usually tell their kid brothers anything."

"But you know," the second brother added, "she did share with us that it really 'creeped her out'. She said there were some kind of initiation rituals that they would have had to take if they wanted to join. She said they didn't want any part of that and never went back."

"Do you know where they went?" said BJ.

"It might have been down around Cowtown, but we're not sure…"

"Well, thanks for this talk, I'll leave you for now. If you think of any other way I can help, please call me." BJ handed the mother a slip of paper with his name and phone number. He headed out the door to his car. *Well, that went somewhat better*, he thought as he headed back into the Pines toward Tuckahoe and Vincent's home.

Staley's was on the way, so he stopped in for lunch before completing his interviews for the day.

Jade was working the room when BJ returned. He sat down at the bar as the bartender presented him with his Seabreeze. Jade came over, smiled warmly and gave him a gentle kiss on the cheek with her arm encircling his waist.

"How'd it go?"

"Difficult at best, the second parent was somewhat more helpful, but I'm not sure I am cut out for interrogation work. There might have been some secretive meeting that all three attended. The brothers mentioned a place called Cowtown. I never heard of that."

"You never heard of Cowtown?" Jade chuckled. "I guess you haven't been here that long. Believe it or not, that's a Rodeo town on the border of Delaware."

"I'm sorry. I'm still a 'rookie' as far as South Jersey is concerned. I'm kinda grasping at straws…I was thinking that we might want to talk more with Justine about what is transpiring at that school. I wonder if she knew any of those three kids?" Jade chose not to respond to him as she disengaged moved back to her hostess chores.

BJ ordered a Reuben without sauerkraut for his lunch. He thought pensively as he drained down his first Seabreeze. Where is this all leading? Is this the path God is taking him down, or is this all just his own doing and will?

When Jade had a free minute she came back to him. "I'm sorry I cut you off before. I'm frankly worried about getting my daughter too much more involved with this. Let me give some additional thought to how Justine can really help us, without getting into any trouble. See what more you can find out about this kid Vincent and fill me in tonight!" Another kiss on the cheek buoyed him. He attacked his sandwich and prepared to head back into the Pines!

He wove us way through the back highways until he got to Tuckahoe. His mind raced through his earlier interviews, the exchange with Jade, and the reemergence of his children in his life. Where was this all taking BJ? He was beginning to find that he enjoyed the investigating more than his teaching? He decided he just needed to focus on the problem at hand and give God a chance to work more in his personal life.

Some more back roads and BJ found himself deep in the pines again. He soon came to the Dinero residence. Much like the area where the Professor lived, this roughhewn cabin-house was among a scattering of similar dwellings deep in the Pines. Two older cars and a tractor were on the property.

He knocked on the door and a deep voice called out, "come in". He stepped into the living room and saw a somewhat older couple sitting at an adjacent dining room table. "You must be that professor from the high school, welcome to our humble abode… This is my wife, Maria, and I am Dean Dinero, Vincent's father. Please sit at our table and enjoy an afternoon snack!" It was charming Italian hospitality—"manga" he expected to hear next.

Dean poured a healthy glass of dark wine, strong than Chianti. BJ thought it might even be homemade. Maria had put out some breads and cheeses with a dipping oil. "What is this about a memorial for our son Vincent?" BJ noted that they didn't seem to have the same sense of despair that he felt in the other homes.

"Thanks for your hospitality, I just wanted to know how we can help you— in any way possible—during this difficult time."

"Thanks for your concern, we honestly didn't think anybody cared about Vincent from that school. He couldn't wait to graduate this June and go to work with his father and brothers. You know, we have a construction firm here in South Jersey. My two older boys work with me on projects from Cape May to Atlantic City. Not bad for an Italian kid who grew up here in the Pines!"

BJ continued to wonder what he had walked into in this particular home. He was at a loss for words. Finally, he thought of something to say or ad: "I know you've been through a lot, but how did Vincent come to be involved with those two girls?"

"We told the police all of this, but they didn't really seem to care. It was like they were just going through the motions. The three of them were just friends who liked to hang out. The girls seemed to look up to my Vincent." Dad was doing all the talking while Maria sat rather passively and nodded her head.

"He met them at the school about a year ago (during his junior year) and they seemed to have a lot of fun together. Vincent even got them involved in some of his clubs—"

"What sort of clubs?"

"We dunno, I think it had to do with music. Vincent always had some strange sort of music that he was listening to. They would go off to some club or meeting once in a while. They always went together."

"Do you know where these 'club' meetings were held?"

"Come to think about it, I think the meetings had something to do with that Rodeo down in Cowtown," offered Dad.

BJ continued the questioning, "Did they get those tattoos together?"

"No, Vincent got his about a year ago, I think he took the girls to one of the Parlors down in Wildwood. The 'Rebel Moon Shop' or something. It might have been about a month ago, around Christmas. I think it was related to those music meetings they were going to. Listen, I don't know what these kids are thinking about these days, I have enough trouble keeping this business together here."

Dad poured BJ another glass of wine, but after the Seabreeze at lunch, he began to feel a little lightheaded.

"Listen, you have been very helpful, the school would like to do anything they can to help you folks out, just give me a call," and BJ gave them another note with his phone number. (Maybe it's time to get some business cards!)

"Funny," said Dad, "I honestly didn't think the school gave a damn— except for that nice man, Mr. Hoover. Vincent seemed real tight with him. We will keep in touch, thanks for caring about him."

As BJ headed back on the road he reflected on his day. Why were the police so nonchalant? He needed to talk with Collins again. Why were two parents deeply upset, and one set of parents not seeming to care? Why and how was Hoover involved with Vincent? How could Justine possibly help with her knowledge of the school?

He also realized that he now had to make a stop at the tattoo parlor in Wildwood. These tattoos and the similarities with the original people living in this area were beginning to come into some focus. He was becoming increasingly concerned about the connections between what was happening at his school and the death of Annie's daughter.

Chapter 18
Back to the Professor – 22 February 2000

Tuesday meant back to the school routine for BJ, even though it was becoming extremely distasteful between Principal Matthew's increasingly bizarre behavior and the continued morose that was growing within the student body. Something was bound to explode! Neither Jade nor BJ could really make sense of the swirling events, so BJ determined to get together with the Todd Collins to try to work facts out. He also thought it might make good sense to get back to Professor Santes who might be able to shed more light on recent events.

It was difficult to keep his thoughts on his classes after the long weekend. When he passed Hoover in the hall he remembered that the Dinero family had mentioned that Hoover was a "friend" of Vincent. This was another avenue he had to explore.

It was late Tuesday afternoon when BJ caught up with Sergeant Todd. Collins was coming off his shift and they tooled down to the local pub to piece together events over a pint or two. BJ was increasingly glad to have made the acquaintance of a like soul. Collins was also coming off a divorce and with two kids in his wife's custody—dealing with the loneliness that creeps in.

By this time, BJ had put his notes into a clear one-page chart with all of the possibilities and dates included. He had gone even further and traced back the career of the three people at Pinelands Regional, Principal Matthews, Vice Principal Martin, and the Math teacher, Hoover. Working at the school, BJ was seeing suspects behind every move and interaction. BJ dramatically put his notes down on the table and leaned over the table and opened up to Collins.

"Todd, the parents of those slain kids…they all seemed to indicate that the 'police didn't really care'. How could that be? What's going on with you guys? Why do the parents feel that way?"

Collins began, "The casinos didn't open until the early 80s, and the NY and Philadelphia cartels both got involved. The small police forces down here are just not really able to handle some of the crimes that occurred. All the murders you found, are, kinda, buried in the 'weeds' of the police records. They never quite got the attention they deserved due to a variety of reasons.

"Local resources and the duplicity of the State Police combine to worsen the problem. This isn't New York City or Los Angeles, violent crimes get kicked up to the State Police and we are more focused on traffic control—then detective work. We do not have the manpower to investigate the kind of conspiracy that you seem to be uncovering here.

"This is not crime TV down here: it's real life! We are more focused on domestic disputes, property fights, and other minor disputes on a daily basis."

"Why weren't the parents of these kids more actively interviewed, investigated, involved?"

"For one, they were mostly poor parents with limited resources. This is not an *OJ* or *Jon Benet Ramsey* caliber. No high-profile cases, just poor backwoods folks for the most part."

"Like Annie's daughter, Kelly: no one was really there to care…"

"Okay," Collins continued, "the victims all seem to be fairly poor—so what could that have had to do with AC and the Mob?"

"Maybe my principal is a key link, he has been in these parts since the mid-80s! Best I can figure he might have some family roots down in Cape May. He had some access to many of these kids, along with that Hoover. I believe that he (Matthews) might have some gambling problems and resulting debts to the mob—that could play into this. And Vice-Principal Martin seems to be an 'odd duck' in the equation!"

"What I can't figure out is this 'cult' issue that you are referring to, BJ. I know you saw something strange with your visit to the Mall, and those kids got away, but there has to be something more."

"That's why I will be exploring the tattoo parlor in Wildwood. I need to see where that image came from and who utilizes it—gangs, cults, whatever. These are some stories that I read, repeated to me by Professor Santes, and related to the tattoos found on many of the bodies. I think we need to get back to him for some additional information. On top of that, I am looking into some contact with the tat parlor!"

"Why do you say WE? What's the point of me coming with you, you've already met him?"

"Todd, you're the professional. Just come in plain clothes, I won't identify you as a cop, just a fellow teacher at the school with an interest in the history of the Pines. Then we can sit down later, over a brew, and try to piece this altogether."

"OK, it makes some sense now that you are involved. I'm beginning to think that a can use an extra, private, hand like yours—within limits—to help us focus on the problem."

BJ pulled the professor's card from his pocket and pulled out his cell phone. The Professor's phone rang several times until his melodious voice answered: "Dr. Santes here, how may I help you?"

He seemed pleasantly surprised to hear BJ's voice and was open to another visit. He almost seemed cheerful to hear that BJ was bringing another teacher friend to feed on the stories of the area.

"Can we come and visit NOW?" replied BJ.

"Sure, BJ, and I look forward to seeing you with your friend."

BJ and Todd quickly jumped into BJ's van and headed out to Santes's cabin. "Let him do most of the talking, Todd, he loves to talk. Perhaps we can get him to speculate on some of our thoughts and ideas."

They headed inland on Route 550, crossing through small towns and pines until they reached the road leading to the Professor's Cabin. BJ still used the rough and crumbled notes he had from the last trip. After one or two missed turns they saw his cabin just up ahead. This time there was no Professor on the front porch. The Cabin appeared deserted. As they left their car to approach the cabin, however, Santes rather suddenly appeared on the front porch. This time he was dressed in a sweater and jacket as if he had just come from a teaching class. But it was the weekend?

"BJ, so good to see you, please introduce me to your friend." The tall man looked down over the other two. Todd extended a hand and a (phony) introduction and Santes invited them both into his rather rustic living room. A bright fire burned in an old stone fireplace against an outside wall.

As he sat in his chair, he reached over into an old, dusty brown box. He fiddled with a latch and popped it open to pull out a box of matches and a pipe from the top portion of the container. He carefully locked the box shut as he prepared his pipe. He excused himself for a minute, got up and left the room.

BJ had wanted a chance to get inside this house, and now that he was there, he carefully observed the room. The main room walls were filled with, what seemed to be, a rather random collection of local prints, historical artwork, and a few sculpted pieces.

In the center of the wall was a fairly large (two feet by three feet) rustic cross. The other pieces seemed to surround the cross. There were additional carvings on the mantle over the fireplace. BJ walked over to peruse them as Santes re-entered the room. They were strange-looking pieces and he would have to take another less conspicuous look at them when he had a chance.

"Please excuse the rather formal attire I was wearing, gentlemen. I was just speaking to a local group of ladies at a church luncheon, and hadn't quite gotten comfortable just yet." Peter was now wearing his familiar poncho and he brought out a plate of cheese and crackers with a pot of tea. Even though the men had both eaten, they politely took part in the late afternoon snack.

"Peter, since we last met and spoke of Kelly's death, you may have heard that three more youth were found near Lake Mummy just after the first of the year. They are reported to have had markings and tattoos on their body similar to what I saw on Kelly."

"I did hear about this when I was at the college last week, and from some of my neighbors. Even the ladies at the church luncheon, this afternoon, were talking quietly about the tragedy. After all, tragedy seems to be a regular part of the history of the Pine Barrens. My topic at the luncheon today was about Emilio Carranza Rodriguez. Do you know about him?"

Both men shook their heads no.

"He was known as the Lindbergh of Mexico. In 1928, they built the 22-year-old exact replica of the Spirit of St. Louis. Carranza's goal was to fly from Mexico City to New York and back again. The trip to New York was accomplished with no problems. But the return flight was fraught with wild thunderstorms, he only go about 50 miles before his plane crashed in the Pine Barrens, just North of Lake Mummy. Legend has it that he had an order in his pocket from a jealous Mexican general who told him to leave immediately.

"A monument was subsequently constructed, helped by the contribution of Mexican school children. It is inscribed in both English and Spanish. The monument contains an Aztec eagle plummeting toward earth along with footprints to signify Carranza's final touch down.

"It is said he still walks among the Pines seeking vengeance on the General who forced him to fly into the storm.

"Sometimes I feel that these deep pines draw heart-ache and tragedy into the midst of these tall trees." He lowered his head as he sipped his tea.

Collins spoke up, "Professor, I am not much of a mystic, but could there be some other connection between Kelly and these three high school students. Is there any kind of cult in this area that is sucking these kids in?"

BJ added, "There has also been talk about the Atlantic City connection between the NYC and Philadelphia Mobs—with interference from Columbian and Mexican drug cartels. I am also wondering if the crime syndicate is involving some of the poorer kids in the Pines."

The Professor stood and began to pace across the cabin floor. He slowly stroked his well-groomed, short beard, as he appeared to be meditating. "BJ, as you know, I have become involved in a number of the clubs and church groups in the area since I moved here. The churches don't seem to be very concerned about drugs and cults. But churches are usually populated by the older generation, so we need to look deeper into the youth movements at work. But I have heard some of the people grumbling about such matters.

"Since the kids now refer to me as 'Black Pieter', perhaps I can 'worm my way in with some of them' to shed more light on this. Have you involved the police yet?"

"No," BJ quickly stammered, "this is just an investigation until we have something to take to them."

"Good, because these young people would get easily spooked by any police involvement. Remember, BJ, the last time you were here I discussed the influence of the Caribbean among the Christian beliefs in this region. We need to focus on what sort of 'practice' are these youth utilizing. Rastafarians (Jamaican-Voodoo-Christians) utilize 'ganja' in their communion ceremonies."

Todd interrupted, "But that was outlawed in Florida, even though they argued 'freedom of religion'."

"Yes, but that won't stop the continued practice."

"Maybe they are substituting cocaine for marijuana in these cults? Possibly obtained from the South American or American mobs. I fear for these kids, they live in the poorest of circumstances, and the traditional school offers them no future. They are obvious targets for any of these groups!" BJ suggested.

"It is certainly worth my exploration, also, I need to look further into the 'Undead' or 'Zombie' influences as well."

At this point BJ had not discussed his seven-year theory. He thought he would leave that for either Todd to suggest, or the Professor to uncover.

"Also, professor, I have my concerns about the Principal of the high school. I think we can become a good team with your help! See what you can find out about him. I'm excited and think we can bring this to a head very soon, for Annie's sake and for the sake of the other kids who have lost their lives."

"Gentlemen, again, thanks for reaching out to me, I am sure I will be able to bring you some additional information in a few weeks. Don't hesitate to call if you have any questions."

BJ's late father wasn't 6'6" or black, but BJ felt especially drawn to the Professor like he had been to his own dad! There was a quiet, somewhat mystical quality to the gentleman—and he was a real gentleman. He really felt a growing bond with that man.

As they drove back toward Route 9, BJ mused that they were in better shape now with a real team of 4! Peter seemed like a real involved and caring leader who could help them reach into the recesses of the culture of the Pines. Todd can continue to lay his hands on police records and BJ can sort of "quarterback" the team toward some solution. He dropped Todd off at the restaurant where they lunched and hurried back to fill in Jade.

After the dinner trade cleared, BJ had time to sit with Jade to debrief her on his afternoon with both Todd and (later) Peter. He was genuinely excited as he filled her in on events. His discoveries, combined with Jade's insight, were beginning to open a small lens on life in the Pines. He just was driven to sort out what specifically had happened to Annie's daughter—and why!

They fell quietly into their quiet corner of Staley's. Annie, working tables instead of streets now, brought them some sandwiches from the closing kitchen and a bottle of Red from the bar. They quietly gathered up their food and drink and moved the meeting upstairs to Jade's apartment. Jade's daughter, Justine, was doing some homework on a desk in the corner.

The long weekend was over for both students and teachers. Her efforts reminded BJ that he still had some preparation to do for his own classes. Maybe this was the time to remind Jade of Justine's possible help. Justine was a student at Pineland Regional, but not, fortunately, in any of his classes.

Jade and BJ talk quietly as they eat at the couch, while Justine continues her studies.

"Jade, I am developing a real fondness with both Sarge and the Professor. I really think we are close to figuring out what is going on in these Pines. Collins is going to research the mob and the possible drug connections. Santes has promised to meet with some of the young people to see if there is any cult involvement.

"Based on what we saw in that Mall, something is going on with these people. These are the same kinds of kids who are disappearing now... And probably over the last 15 years.

"I'm still not convinced if any or all of these killings and disappearances are directly connected. The 'Jersey Devil' and a plane crash in the Pinelands simply add to the mystery that have been promulgated by those who want to bring more vacationers and sightseers into this area. What could Kelly have to do with any of this?"

"But BJ, how do we explain the continued appearances of this tricolored tattoos with the cross in the center. Kelly had those on her body. And we saw the markings on those kids in the Mall."

"And I'm still wondering about both, Matthews, Martin, and Hoover. Something is going on there."

Justine raised her head from her desk and turned toward them. Without prompting, she offered her views: "Those three all creep me out along with a bunch of my friends. But I have noticed that some of these fringe kids seem to hang around with Hoover. Matthews just seems like a middle-aged letch, who thinks he's cool. Hoover seems to spend as much time with the young boys as he does the young girls. Vice-Principal Martin just seems to hang out ogling girls."

She was a bright young woman on the road to a college scholarship. Like her mother, she was sharp and perceptive. They welcomed her into the conversation.

"Justine, all of this stays right between all three of us, OK?"

"Sure BJ, I get it, I hardly see you at that big high school, but when I do, it's always 'Mr. Gleeson'. There is a group of kids who seem to be real outsiders, dressing in black, with lots of piercings. They're not involved in anything at the school: Real quiet in classes. I have seen Hoover with some of them, in the cafeteria mostly."

"Jade, if it's OK with you, I'd like to make Justine my 'unofficial undercover deputy' as we continue our investigation. The kids won't really open up with me, but I bet they will with her!"

Jade had previously been reticent to agree, but Justine was chomping at the bit to get involved. After some discussion, she was on board. The team was now up to five, if BJ included Justine. Jade would not let go of her concerns without insisting! "BJ, you better make sure nothing happens to her."

BJ responded: "I'm still not sure what we are doing. I will protect her. Does any of this really matter? Does old Annie appreciate what they were trying to do for her?"

"Of course she does," offered Jade. "She is almost totally clean now and beyond grateful for the efforts you are taking."

Jade encouraged Justine to retire to her room. BJ and her finished their bottle of wine and began to plan their next steps. Justine will do her snooping at school. The Professor will begin to look into his neighborhood youth. Collins will get better insight on some of those older incidents and police records.

BJ planned to follow up with Matthews, Martin, and Hoover when school resumed tomorrow. Events were coming to a head. BJ thought he could see the proverbial "light at the end of the tunnel". He just couldn't be sure that it wasn't the lights of another train!

As he was driving home, he decided to call Carly. She answered on the first ring, "Hi Dad."

"Look, I know it's short notice, but how about if I meet you in Dover for lunch tomorrow around 1:00 PM?"

"Aren't you working, Dad?"

"Yes, but I'm going to pull a sick day. I have an appointment in Wildwood in the late afternoon and I thought I would come down to see you first."

"Dad, it will have to be a relatively short lunch, but I will be glad to come out to meet you. There is a neat diner right on the main highway, just off from the military morgue and my college. I'll text you directions and see you at noon! I am looking forward to seeing you again."

"I'll be there," responded BJ, who promptly hung up and pulled into his driveway. He felt that he was in the real process of reorganizing his life!

Chapter 19
Wildwood and Beyond – 23 February 2000

BJ had scheduled his visit to the Tattoo parlor for later on Wednesday afternoon. But after his decision to play hooky, he was now heading down to Dover, Delaware, to have lunch with his daughter. Then he would head back North with a stop-off at Wildwood.

He weaved us way through Southern New Jersey for almost one hour until he finally found the Delaware Memorial Bridge. After that, he located Route 13 and it was a straight shot to the state capitol. He found the Tri-State Diner that Carly had picked right on the corner toward the center of town.

His heart skipped a beat as he saw his daughter standing just outside the Diner door. He almost found himself running across the parking lot. He hadn't seen her since last Thanksgiving and he was almost adjectively sorry for his own poor behavior!

They embraced, tearfully, and walked arm in arm into the diner.

"Dad, it's been far too long. I thought I had lost you forever."

"Carly, it's on me, I have been lost. I am in the process of finding myself. Except I have myself mired in a developing criminal investigation. In fact I have to go back to Wildwood this evening to interview the owner of a tattoo parlor. So I'm still kinda lost. I thought I wanted to be a teacher and a coach and now I'm being drawn into some type of amateur detective work—and liking it. But you always knew your dad was just a bit flaky and also overly curious."

"Yeah, I guess I always did. But now I just want to tell you all about me and find out more about you!"

As they were sitting down, BJ began to provide Carly with all the gory details of his current investigation. He also filled her in, gently, on his current relationship. He cut short his story so he could listen to her. They sat down a nice meal, Carly ordered a Cobb salad and BJ settled for a pastrami sandwich on rye. They both had unsweetened ice tea.

Carly went first and told BJ about her decision to be a doctor until she recognized the years it would take. She then found some friends who had gone the PA route. They were truly in love with what they did, making some good money, and it didn't take eight years and $200,000! Her internship was at the military base in Dover.

"They have a special military morgue in Dover. That's where all the bodies from overseas come, like Iraq and Afghanistan. It might sound creepy, but I get to do anatomical studies on some of the corpses."

"Wow, I'm impressed, sounds really interesting. I'm rather surprised that you have moved into this career area."

"Well, Dad, you never were really close to me through high school. Now, maybe, we can get closer."

BJ winced, and then continued: "Carly, I won't make promises I cannot keep, but I can tell you that I will do all within my power to stay closer to you. Let's make 'once a month' a rule from now on."

Carly teared up. "Dad, it is so good to be with you again. I can't wait till we repeat this!"

They walked out to the parking lot, BJ hugged her closely, they both stepped back and saw the tears as they turned and entered their respective cars.

From here, BJ headed out for the Rebel Moon Shop in Wildwood. It took him about another hour to get from Dover to Wildwood. The shop itself was located on the boardwalk in North Wildwood. BJ parked on a side street and strolled down the empty boardwalk until he reached the store.

Although he was a beach fanatic, it had been some time since BJ had walked the boardwalk in Wildwood. He thought back to his parent's visit to this place back in 1964! He was pushing 14 at the time. A new tune was moving to the top of the popular tunes of the day. The Drifters had just published *Under the Boardwalk*. BJ always seemed to have a tune in his head; but on this day, at this time *under the boardwalk* sounded strange.

Why under the boardwalk? What were they trying to do or hide: making love, cooling your feet? He always felt that the song sounded sad. He later discovered that the song was recorded the day after one of their members had died suddenly. That accounted for the melancholy sound to what would have been an upbeat beach tune.

As he walked, the tune languished in his head. He looked around at the frivolity that was taking place, even in the off season. Not a crowd, but people still strolled with the setting sun, hand in hand. *Why am I letting this sadness get to me*, he thought, *but there are always things going on that we cannot see—hidden*. What was being hidden through all of this? What more could he uncover with his travels and interviews? Where was this taking him—and did he even want to go to wherever "where" was!

Despite his meandering thoughts, BJ came up upon the shop. The tattoo parlor generally bustled during the summer months, but they still had a rather steady trade—even in the doldrums of February. There were three stations in the darkly lite studio. He had called in advance and spoken to Eddie, who was the owner.

He didn't give away his hand, just said he wanted to speak with him for an article he was writing for an area magazine, *Exit Zero*. BJ had seen copies of this rather upbeat magazine that focused on the Wildwood area. He hoped that it would give him a better "in" with which to feel out the owner.

There were only two people in the shop when BJ entered. Eddie welcomed him but asked him to wait while he finished up with a client. BJ had never gone the tattoo route and never even been in a tattoo shop. He found the procedures rather fascinating. Eddie was finishing up a butterfly on the lower leg of a young woman. She seemed relaxed and not in pain.

BJ didn't know what kind or if there was pain in the process. He just knew that these kids he was investigating had all come here for the procedure. When he had finished up, Eddie brought BJ to his office in the back. BJ cut right to the chase, he took a scrap of paper out of his pocket that had a recreation of the multi-colored cross image that he had seen.

"Have you seen this particular image here or do you offer it?"

"Yeah, I've seen that and done that!" offered Eddie. "About a year ago, a few dudes came in here and showed this to me. I'm an artist—so I obliged."

BJ continued, "Did they show it to you from a book or a photo?"

"They were showing me a photo of the arm of a black dude. The image was clear in the photo, so I used that as my guide.

"All six of them got the ink that night. They asked me to keep the image on file because they would be sending some friends. Over the year, I bet I had about 20-25 requests. Must be some kind of a club or something?"

"Did you keep a copy of that photo? Do you keep records?"

"Yeah (kinda), we are required to keep records primarily for health and safety, but we always recognize the confidentially of our clients. I might have the original photo in a file back here."

"Can you at least share information on this particular tat?"

"I dunno, I thought you were just here to write an article?"

"I am, but a good writer has to put some 'meat on the bones', you know, like, expand a bit." BJ went on to provide a bit more data. He talked about Vincent's mother who gave him the name of the shop. He asked if he remembered Vincent.

"Yeah, I remember him, nice kid, he brought in a number of people for the same artwork. That was just a few months after the initial group got inked!"

"Do you know that Vincent is dead?"

"No…are you an investigator or something…what's going on here?"

BJ went on to explain that he was simply trying to origin of this symbol. That it was, indeed, a part of an investigation that had nothing to do with Eddy. It was really for BJ to find out more about the people who brought him this image to reproduce.

Eddy was somewhat relieved yet still concerned. "Can we continue this discussion at the bar across the boardwalk, I don't want any of my customers or co-workers hearing any of this."

"Sure," said BJ, "I'm buying."

They settled into a corner booth and BJ bought a round of beers for both of them.

"Look," said Eddie, "I got a nice boardwalk business going here. I'll help you with some information, but it's got to be kept quiet. My clients do want their privacy."

"I fully understand, Eddie. It's just that almost seven people have ended up murdered and they all had your artwork. I'm not involving you, I just need to know who brought you the initial art."

"The initial group that brought the art was made up of about five young people and one older woman. The leader was a tall black woman with striking features. An older man was with them who just stood quietly and watched. I inked the five young people who were there. I have all their names back in the shop. The older gentleman picked up the tab for all of them. Then within the year Vincent came in a few times bringing some young people for the same piece. The last time he came in with two nice high school girls.

"It was funny, neither girl had ever had a tattoo, and they were nervous and giggling at the same time. But Vincent told them that's what it would take to make them a member of the 'club'."

"Eddie, did they say what sort of a club?"

"No, and they kinda clammed up when I asked them about it."

BJ went back to the shop with Eddie. He went back into his office to retrieve the records. "I have the names and addresses of the five young people; strange but I can't find any of the information on the older gentleman. Maybe 'cause he didn't get the tattoo and he paid in cash. I did find the original photo of the image that you can have." Eddie handed the list and the crumpled photo over to BJ.

"Would you recognize any of this group or the leader if you saw them again?" asked BJ.

"Honestly, I don't know, I see so many different people in the shop."

BJ thanked Eddy for the information and headed to his parked van. He reflected on what sort of a group had been formed. He wondered about the older man who paid for the tattoos. Could it have been Matthews? *Damn, though BJ, I never asked him for a description of the older dude.*

When he got back to his apartment he pulled out the list that he had been given and put his notes of the visit together. The names and addresses made no initial sense to him and he put them aside for future checking and reference. BJ now had a real photo of an arm carrying the tattoo symbol. This was definitely connected to some sort of organization or cult. This was something to bring back to the professor as soon as possible. BJ bet that Santes would be able to identify its background.

He began to move his Van out to the Parkway for the 30-minute or so ride back to Sea Isle. He put his XM car radio on for some company on the ride home—and to clear his head. But to his surprise, *Under the Boardwalk* came up on a 60's station and he had to listen to the Drifters with their bittersweet rendition. It made him think of what lies were under these "boards" he is treading on. When he really begins to lift them up, what will he really find?

He turned off the radio and continued home in silent reflection.

Chapter 20
The Mob Emerges – 24 February 2000

BJ stopped at the tavern to fill in Jade before heading back to Sea Isle. BJ didn't get back to his apartment until way after 2:00 AM. She continued to be supportive of his efforts, and also, continued to be concerned about both his welfare and Justine's. It wasn't just a discussion of the murder—but developed into another passionate encounter. BJ was getting worried about his deepening involvement, but it didn't seem to faze Jade. He quickly put some lesson plans in place and fell asleep—fitfully around 3!

As he drove into the parking lot, he had concocted an excuse to see Principal Matthews after school. It would have to do with the start of baseball practice on 1 March. He was sharing a cup of coffee with "Crab" in the faculty room when the Principal's secretary came in and presented BJ with a formal letter. She said nothing, turned on her heels, and walked out.

BJ couldn't wait to get out of the faculty room to a more private space to open the letter. It startled him!

Dear Mr. Gleeson:
I need to see you at 3:30 PM this afternoon to discuss a matter of importance relative to a pending board action relative to your employment for the 2000-2001 school year.
Failure to attend this meeting could result in your immediate suspension and/or termination.

Sincerely,
Clark Matthews, EdD.

What was going on? He had received superlative classroom reviews from his department chairperson. Matthews had never been in his classroom. Certainly his dismal record in baseball last year could result in his termination as coach—but not as a teacher. There was nothing he could do, for now, but wait until the end of the day. What had gone south with what was becoming a blossoming professional relationship?

The day dragged on forever.

He called Jade just after lunch: "Jade, you can't believe what is happening!" He read her the memo and she was equally surprised.

"Watch what you say to him, BJ."

"I can keep my cool when I need to, but I'm worried I might lose it!"

"I have faith in you, BJ, do this for Annie and Kelly, but more important keep yourself safe. You are becoming very important to me and—I must add—Justine."

"Thanks, I needed that, I'm glad I called. I will talk to you after the meeting."

BJ had a free period just prior to the end of the day, so he tried to anticipate what was going on. No success as he played mind games with what he knew about Matthews and Atlantic City. Perhaps his involvement with the three murdered students had gotten back to Matthews? He spent the next 20 minutes grading papers to take his mind off the pending meeting. Just before he went to see Matthews, however, he decided to call officer Collins.

After four or five rings, Collins picked up, recognizing BJ's number.

"I don't know what I've gotten myself into, but I am getting very nervous," BJ offered as he filled Collins in on the events of the morning.

"Just keep your cool and listen! Don't commit or admit to anything. Sometimes a memo like that is just to get your attention. Call me when you're done."

At 3:30, he headed into the Principal's outer office. The secretary was busy at her desk, but he was surprised to see Will Hoover sitting in another chair reading a magazine. Matthews opened his office door and invited BJ inside. BJ was surprised that VP Martin was already there.

"Don't be upset with the letter we gave you this morning. We may be faced with a budget crunch and we had to cover our asses by giving all our non-tenured teachers the same letter. This is a mandatory letter called a 'Rice Letter' that our attorneys require us to send at times like this."

BJ breathed a huge sigh of relief!

He continued, "I just thought this would be a good time to catch up on some other situations. Would you mind if I brought Will Hoover in here to join us?"

BJ shrugged. He was rather surprised, but this might be playing right into his hands. Why would he want Hoover in the room just now? On the other hand, maybe events are working out on behalf of his "team". Through all this, Martin just sat and quietly observed.

"No, whatever works for you."

Matthews got up, went to the door, and motioned Hoover into the room. Hoover sat across the room, glaring at BJ.

"We both talked back in early January about that little scene with Will, Martin and I at the casino."

"Yeah, I remember…but that didn't seem like a big deal. I was focused on the big guy that got into the brawl and was arrested by the cops."

"Well, our situation has heated up somewhat, and we want to make sure whose side you are on if the proverbial 'shit hits the fan'. There have been some inquiries from the Feds about our relationships in AC, and now with the murder of some of our students—"

"What do I have to do with any of this?"

"I am getting concerned that you are becoming more of a detective than a teacher. Word is that you have been meeting with Sergeant Collins from the State police and that you have been speaking to some students hear at the school. I also had some negative feedback from the parents of Ruth about your visit to their home. You claimed to be representing me?"

"Todd's just a casual friend and as for the murdered kids—well, I just wanted to see if the school could help in some way…nobody seems to really care about those kids. But I do!"

"OK, I'll take you at your word. But you have to stay totally away from any and all of this. Is that understood?"

BJ was trying to be meek and mild, "I'll try—"

"Trying isn't good enough. You must cease and desist. In the meantime, I would like to meet with you off campus tonight to further clarify the role that Hoover, Martin, and I are playing in this investigation. There is more here than meets the average eye. As a result, we want to meet you with some of our associates at Old Murphy's Irish Pub in Millville. It's just off 347. Dinner is on us, and perhaps we can bring any concerns you may have to a resolution.

"See you at 8!" Matthews stood up and escorted BJ to the door. Hoover and Martin stayed behind as he walked back into his office.

BJ was temporarily stunned. He quickly went back to Staley's to fill in Jade. On his way back, he called Collins who was still on desk duty back at the barracks.

"This is getting too far out of control. Not only has he seemed to figure out my involvement, but also he wants to pull me in on whatever scam he is involved in from that Atlantic City affair! He also seems to know that you and I are involved. I don't know what I'm going to do…"

Collins replied, "He might just be guessing, but since he saw you on New Year's Eve, he may be worried how much more you know. In any respect, I would be very careful meeting those guys alone. They might be trying to buy you off—or seriously scare you off or even worse. I better 'tail' your car tonight for extra protection. It sounds like he is playing his cards real close to his chest. Vaguely threatening you, but at the same time holding out an 'olive branch' for redemption and resolution.

"It almost sounds like he is still trying to pull you into that inner circle. An inner circle you most probably want to avoid!"

"That's what has me worried too, Todd. I confess that I am just a little nervous walking in on this 'special' supper tonight. It's also," continued BJ, "a fairly out of the way restaurant he is inviting me to. This is beginning to smell like fish left on the beach in the sun."

"Don't worry, BJ, I've got your back. Just keep me posted all the way."

"Thanks Todd, it's comforting having you at my back! Why don't you meet me at Staley's at 7 so we can wend our way to the restaurant?"

BJ's mind was racing as he worked his way back to Staley's. He was no longer a loner! He had to count on other people to get him through this mess. Jade, Todd, Justine, and Peter were all there for him. He had never experienced this sort of camaraderie except with some of his minor league teams—where players bonded and hung together.

He now began to perceive himself in a very different role. He was no longer "coach" or "teach", he was finding himself thrust into situations to which he had never been exposed. He was being forced to perform tasks he had never experienced. But, through all the change and even danger: he felt a sense of exhilaration that he could never remember experiencing.

Even his minor league no-hitter lacked the intensity that this current problem provided for him. With all the anxiety that he currently experienced, he had a sense of calm, comfort and satisfaction that was uncommon to his old persona.

Jade saw BJ enter and moved quickly, if not running, to him. She embraced him tightly and shared her concerns and worries about the rapidly unfolding events. BJ filled in Jade on the afternoon meeting but she, too, was frightened for BJ, until he told her that Collins would be following him. That relieved her somewhat. BJ noticed that Pine-Bog Annie was waiting tables in their area.

Apparently, Jade had done a remarkable job helping her sober up and get past the loss of her daughter! When she had a chance, she sat down between BJ and Jade.

"You know I overheard you talking about that Principal Matthews. I think my Kelly knew him in some way. While we were both still turning tricks, Kelly told me about this creepy Principal who was always working the bars and corners looking to score. She had dropped out, but he had a bad rep, even with the other 'girls'."

"Thanks Annie, this gives me even more to think about. Jade, this is even more for Justine to look into as she interacts with the students at Pinelands Regional."

As they continued to talk, Sergeant Collins walked in, plain-clothed. He came over and sat down with them.

"I've been checking the wires and sheets coming in from AC and other surrounding areas. This mob interaction seems to be heating up—particularly with the Columbian group. Watch what you say to these characters this evening over supper. Also, don't lose me on the way to and from the restaurant."

They got into their respective cars and headed out on Route 47 to the intersection of 347 that took BJ right into Millville with Collins trailing about 3 cars behind. *Collins must be very practiced at this*, thought BJ.

As BJ pulled into the parking lot of the Irish pub, he noticed two rather pretentious black limousines in the back of the parking lot. The windows seemed darkened, but there appeared to be people inside. A large man in a dark suit was standing outside of one of the limos smoking a cigarette. When he entered the pub, he found Mathews, Martin, and Hoover at a quiet booth in the far back of the restaurant portion.

He sat down next to the three men. They had empty glasses in front of them and seemed to have had several stiff drinks already. A waiter was producing another round. Matthews had ordered an Irish whiskey (neat) for him.

"Let's get down to brass tacks," began Matthews. "What we say here stays here. Your presence at that bar on New Year's Eve put you in a really bad position. You had no reason to understand that there were some really bad dudes involved with us. Honestly, both of us (looking at Hoover) got in over our heads, but there is light at the end of the tunnel and a pot of gold under the rainbow. Now that you're IN, you can be a part of the profit.

"But you really must cease and desist from any more investigation into Kelly or any of those other kids who disappeared."

"How do you know Kelly?" offered BJ.

"I have had my experience with the AC hookers, and Kelly was a classy one. But she got in over her head—and you know what happened to her! Those other kids just ended up in the wrong place at the wrong time."

"I'm not sure what you guys are offering me—or trying to scare me about. Kelly's mom has become a friend of mine. That's why I got involved. But what 'pot of gold' are you even talking about?"

Hoover began to speak, "The cocaine train has arrived in the Pines, anyone who meets it at the station can set themselves up for life. There is an active waiting audience right here where nobody cares—"

"Shut up, Hoover, you're moving too fast for BJ here." Through all of this, Martin just sat quietly looking around the room.

BJ couldn't believe what he was hearing. It was all unfolding in front of him. He literally didn't know what to say or which way to turn. Before he even would even begin to try to answer, he excused himself to go to the men's room, mainly to collect his thoughts. While he was there, he pulled out his cell phone and filled Collins in on the developments.

Collins got back to him: "Watch yourself, BJ, and watch what you say, by the way I saw some very unsavory dudes with long coats and black hats who just moving toward the restaurant. Stay in the bathroom for a minute until I call you back."

BJ's phone hummed quietly. It was Collins: "I just saw VP Martin come out and meet the 'men in black' and is escorting them back into the restaurant. Come out of the room very slowly and deliberately."

BJ took the advice and slowly emerged from the men's room door. He looked around the corner carefully, to see an empty table with Hoover and Matthews being herded out of the restaurant by Martin and about four men that seemed to match the description that Collins gave him. He stayed where he was and quietly went to the door only to see the men being pushed into the back of a limo that was trying to exit a busy parking lot.

He quickly moved to his car and saw Collins in his car parked on the other side of the lot. Martin gets into a different car and heads out first. The limo is heading downtown toward Route 347. Martin turns and exits in a different direction. BJ quickly goes over to Collins and they agree to follow the limo, with Collins following BJ.

He catches up with the limo a few blocks over but slows down. BJ is no expert at following but tracks them pretty well down 347 toward Rt. 47 South. By now the roads are pretty empty and Collins is blinking his lights to slow BJ down. But they hit a light just before Rt. 47 and the limo speeds up and disappears on the empty road.

"I think we lost them," BJ said as he and Collins stopped and exited their car in the lot of a Dunkin Donuts.

"BJ, we have to be very careful about any further involvement. We really are in over our heads in this affair. I could be in deep trouble with my department and you could be in even worse trouble with your job!"

After a few minutes, they jump back in their respective cars and head toward home on the same route (47) that they took to get to the restaurant.

About three miles down the road, they see the black limo, partially on a shoulder and hanging down an embankment. There are state police cars with their light flashing at the scene. Two ambulances have already arrived.

Collins and BJ pull up near the scene and walk over toward the embankment together. Collins shows his badge and introduces himself to his fellow state policemen. That allows both of them to informally look over the scene. BJ is trying to look very inconspicuous—but it's probably not working.

BJ and Collins look into the car but no one is there. Further down the hill, they see only a body that is covered by an ambulance blanket. The body appears to been burned and charred beyond recognition. Collins motions for

BJ to hang back while he goes in to examine the body. There is clearly a missing hand on the victim but no sign of it in the immediate area. The State Police that they have just been on the scene for a minute or so!

Quickly taking advantage of the confusion, Collins and BJ looked over the scene. There was evidence of other car tracks, multiple footprints, and one clear indication of a high-heeled woman's boot.

Collins told BJ, "Get out of here right now. I will follow up with our department, but you shouldn't be seen here anymore than this."

He heads back to see Jade before he heads home, on the way he checks his cell phone. In the turmoil, he has missed a call from Jade.

"BJ, I got an interesting phone call from your friend, the professor. He called me and would like to meet with Justine and me. You suggested he is 'one of the team'—so I agreed. Can't wait to hear about tonight from you."

Boy, thought BJ, *Do you want to hear about this*!

Twenty minutes later, he found himself in a deep embrace with Jade. He had gotten back to Staley's by around 11 and the weekday crowd resulted in an almost empty bar. He filled her in on the events and she trembled when he spoke of the car crash and the 'men in black'. Was this ending or was it just beginning? He never made it back to Sea Isle that night; the embrace with Jade, once again, continued in the room upstairs over Staley's.

Chapter 21
The Onion Snow – March 2000

Time flew by for BJ over the next few weeks. His high school was in a state of turmoil over the death of a teacher and the disappearance of Principal Mathews. Events seemed to be all collapsing in over him. Despite the season!

It was the beginning of March and the Pines were subjected to what the farmers call "Onion Snow". That usually is the last snow of the winter, it falls fast and hard, but it doesn't last. And the Jersey farmers know it's time to plant the onions! It's the first planting of the new season. High School Baseball practice officially begins in New Jersey and, with everything else going on, BJ was in the early stages of identifying if he could improve his team for this year.

A light snow had fallen over the region. It would be gone in a day or so, but it put a different mood in the seaside air! BJ was becoming increasingly involved in what now appeared to be ritualistic killings. He was still trying to determine the connection between the high school and these murders. On top of this, the spring is fraught with new relationship problems for BJ. He is getting closer and closer to Jade; but now his own children have popped back into the picture and he is concerned with his balancing act.

The investigation of the February "accident" determined that it was the body of Hoover. Principal Matthews was listed as missing—and presumed dead. The Vice-Principal, Martin, apparently was not with them and showed up for school as if everything was normal. He was named Acting Principal by the Board of Education. These events had already cast a pall over the high school celebration of Valentine's Day and the surrounding communities. Now it was more about the dead kids than the missing administrator and one dead teacher!

The press from Atlantic City was citing his gambling debts and mob involvement for the murder. The cynics who didn't like Matthews anyway were saying, "I told you so", while those few who supported or didn't know Matthews were deeply saddened and troubled. There was little concern over the un-liked teacher, but four deaths in a high school within two months were hard for anyone to fathom. Staff were surprised that Martin had been appointed to finish out the school year. He seemed to have walked away from all of this scot-free.

Over the past week, Collins and BJ were jumping through proverbial hoops in their own respective jobs. Collins was questioned for his involvement the night of the car death of Hoover. What was he doing in that area and, furthermore, why did he become involved in checking for footprints and other evidence. Collins simply said he had a night off and was with a friend (BJ). In spite of his protestations, he was under heavy scrutiny from his own department.

The atmosphere at the school was further toxic. No one seemed to understand what was happening and students began to huddle together in small groups all over the campus. Principal Martin reaction was particularly disturbing to BJ. It was becoming clear to students and staff alike that their history teacher/baseball coach was seriously looking into this situation. One day, he asked to meet, privately, with BJ.

"I just wanted to privately explain my 'presence' at the dinner last month," said Martin, "You need to know that I was there on behalf of the board of education. That is a private and confidential piece of information. I had let the Board President know about the meeting and asked me to report back. With the disappearance of Matthews, the Board has asked that this matter be kept private.

"This includes you," Martin continued. "You will notice I just sat and listened, I didn't add anything to the conversation. I had to leave early, while you were in the bathroom, and before those thugs rousted Matthews and Hoover. I was as surprised as you were with the comments that Matthews made. I further appreciate that you never mentioned any agreement to any of that stated nonsense."

"What about the police?" asked BJ. "Didn't they question you?"

"Sure, the next day, and I fully cooperated with them."

"Well, how does this affect my role here at the school, now that you are the Principal?"

"Just keep quiet, listen to what the police have to tell you, and you'll do just fine. Too many people are questioning your involvement in this situation. Just concentrate on being a baseball coach and a teacher. Leave the investigative work to the professionals!"

BJ left Martin even further confused. BJ was now being included in much of the discussions with police due to the intervention of his hew buddy, Todd. BJ needed to further sort things out, so once school was out for the day, and baseball practice over, it was time for some additional Ocean Reflection, so BJ found himself walking the beach at Strathmere (again).

Once again, he picked up individual shells, looked at them, and tossed them back into the waves. One at a time! He had enough shells at his apartment to last a lifetime. He needed to put all of this into the hands of the God that he worshiped, but still felt he was either separated or at a distance from that God. Part of that was the insecurity that had always dogged BJ.

He realized that he was at an important junction in his life. Where was this taking him? What about this new relationship? What was the status of his job? How can he become 'more' to his children? Why was the investigatory procedure more interesting than his history classes? His mind swirled as he strolled along the sand.

At least he had opened up a good dialogue with both of his children. It even made his ex-wife, Cassie, somewhat calmer toward him. He was equally perplexed, confused, and yet excited about what his future held for him.

But, he had to help get through this mystery that had fallen into the lap of both Jade and himself. He owed it to Annie. It was time for the "team" to reassemble. Jade was a great help, Todd was BJ's link to the real detectives, the Professor held a lot of knowledge of the Pines—which probably will prove valuable to BJ.

He prolonged his beach walk so he could better plan the meeting that lied just ahead. He needed to be a good leader with all of them. Even so, he was treading into areas he had never known before—but enjoying it immensely. He was a good careful thinker and planner. He also fully enjoyed any kind of puzzles... So he needed to utilize these skills over the next few weeks. But his empathetic side needed some real improvement. How he reacted to all the people surrounding him just now was critical.

James and Carly needed to see a more caring side of him. Conversely, Jade was beginning to wonder what was happening with their relationship. Vice-

Principal Martin wanted him to back off, but Todd Collins was encouraging his involvement.

So he took one last look at the waves, shook the sand from his shoes, and headed back to his apartment where he would kick back, pour a nice jigger of Irish whiskey and try to just plain relax (which he was not very good at doing...) Then it hit him, it was the onset of Lent and tomorrow was Ash Wednesday. This rang a quiet bell deep inside BJ's brain, but he ignored it as he headed out for his meeting with his "team".

Jade, BJ, Collins, and Annie were together again commiserating over events. They had invited the Professor to join them, but he said he was involved with several major church groups in his area and would have to wait for a separate visit from Jade and Justine. BJ walked into Staley's with a large bag that he tossed casually on the table. Collins and Jade were drinking their pints and looked up at him, rather startled.

"Happy Fat Tuesday,", exclaimed Gleeson.

Today marks the last day before the beginning of Lent. It's a time when the people in New Orleans really let go. They get to splurge and party before the penitence of Lent hits them on Ash Wednesday. These are fachnacts—a donut that the Pennsylvania Dutch introduces every year at this time to 'celebrate' fat Tuesday. They are loaded with calories...truly fattening.

Annie was downing her third cup of black coffee. Jade had scheduled a meeting with Professor Santes, but that wasn't for another week or so.

"I was beginning to think that Matthews and Hoover were directly involved in these deaths, but it appears that this might have been just a sideshow for the mob battles over drugs," offered BJ.

"My sources indicate that the Columbians have taken over the cocaine trade in this part of the Pines and are in a state of war with the Philadelphia Mob. The people investigating," said Collins.

"Where was Matthews? Had he been killed and removed to another location?"

"Are these just young people being caught in the cocaine epidemic?" said Jade.

BJ continued, "But there was no cocaine readily available here 15 years ago, and these killings were still apparently happening. And what about the strange tattoos and severed body parts (fingers and hands)? It's got to be something more, but I can't figure out what. What's more, there seems to be a time gap between what are looking, more and more, like ritualistic killings…"

"Yes," said Jade, "and between Christmas and Easter!" They all stared at her. Then that quiet bell in BJ's head rang again. He recognized it this time. Most all of the murders had occurred during that Lenten time period. The coroner's office determined Kelly's death for some time in August. Also, the three recent high school students seemed to have occurred just prior to the onset of Lent. There were a few other exceptions, but it seemed that BJ's historical research in the area did put those recent murders in the window of Lent.

"The new church year," began BJ, "begins shortly after Christmas and moves clearly into Lent based on some rather ancient calendars. People mark the beginning of Lent with Ash Wednesday (and Fat Tuesday), for centuries. The actual dates of Easter triggers the beginning of Lent. Easter falls on the first Sunday following the first full moon after the vernal equinox!

"Therefore, Lent and Easter fall on different dates every year. But most of these murders have fallen into the season of Lent! This is more than just a coincidence!"

*****

Another week later, after the "team talks", somewhere south of them, a State Trooper from Collin's barracks is making a routine patrol of a combined camp-ground and rest stop on the Garden State Parkway. He pulled into the parking grounds and got out to walk toward the rest rooms.

As he walks, he notices what seem to be bloodstained footprints coming into the clearing. The trooper follows the path into a clearing in a small copse of trees. Here he finds a crude form of an altar with cheap imitation silver goblets. Nearby are some sharp and pointed tools that remind the trooper of dissection knives.

At this point, the Trooper calls for backup. Sergeant Collins decides to join the crew going to the scene. As the group begins to fan out into the area, they find more evidence of blood spills and a strange snow angel silhouette in the snow that makes police believe there had been a body in that space.

The strangest part of the scene, however, is that while there are footprints into the clearing and the altar, there are no footprints leading out!

Chapter 22
Justine's Involvement – Mid-March, 2000

Later that month, Collins called BJ at school to inform him of the new discovery. He arranged to meet Collins at Staley's in the early evening to fill him in.

"This is really getting strange, it freaked out the trooper and the contingent that came to the scene, there were no footprints leading out? Maybe the Jersey Devil just flew out of the clearing," said Collins jokingly.

"This confirms our growing belief that this is ritualistic in nature—and calendar-driven—not just the Jersey Devil flying around and causing mayhem and havoc!"

"Odd though, there was no body to be found, just blood on the snow."

"Are there any reports at your headquarters about missing persons?"

"Not at this point, then again, folks in this area don't really get concerned if their kid disappears for a few days. When they do report to some authority, they get told to wait awhile. We are not as careful in the country as the cops in the cities, even Atlantic City is better."

"How about Matthews, has he surfaced anywhere?"

"No reports to date of his whereabouts."

As they continue to ruminate over the incident, Justine came into the tavern from school. Justine was beginning to resemble a butterfly emerging from a cocoon. School had not really turner her on and she was still struggling with the loss of her father when she was about 10 years old. Jade was not always able to give her the attention she needed and the school did nothing to help her develop and grow!

Justine was supportive of Jade and BJ's relationship. Her parents' problems had soured her on relationships and even though she was a beauty that took after her mother, at this point there were no serious boyfriends—and no dating.

BJ was emerging as a sort of father figure for her. Her involvement in Kelly's case really began to change her for the better. BJ could actually feel her positive energy as she tried to help with the case. Maybe he wasn't such a bad guy after all—he thought. Justine was quite yet bright. She was escaping into her studies as a way of sorting out her own life. Like BJ, she was pretty much a loner.

She tossed her books on the table where they were sitting and sat down with them. BJ had noticed that she was getting more and more concerned about this problem. Even though she wasn't highly involved in school activities, it was HER high school. It was her classmates who had died! Now the principal was missing! Add to this, she knew that her mom's boyfriend was trying to help Pine-Bog Annie find out what had happened to Kelly, who she indirectly knew.

After listening carefully to the discussion, Justine finally jumps into the conversation:

"Well, if I am your school undercover snoop, you better pay some attention to what I have been observing. Most of this was school scuttlebutt, but it's beginning to come into focus some sense now these events are unfolding. I've been doing some serious listening"—she held up a folder stuffed with papers—"These are all the notes I have put together so far. It's pretty hard to separate truth for fiction, particularly in a school lunch room!

"Over the past few weeks, I began to sit at different tables in the cafeteria and just kinda 'listen'. Tables in school cafeterias are so predictable. Most kids gravitate to their "interest" table, be it sports, theatre, band, or cheerleading. Our school also breaks out into regional groups—neighborhoods. We are so big that it's really hard to make friends outside of a very small group."

BJ looked at the list of notes Justine had taken down. He was surprised at how carefully she had categorized the comments that she heard. She carefully noted the name of the student, their regional area, and a few other notes about their appearance. What she was uncovering was clearly the sign of a dysfunctional school culture...but the signs of murder and violence?

"I remember, about a month or so ago, a group of kids—the gothic types—were laughing it up around a cafeteria table. One of the kids was showing off a small box to the others who were whooping and hollering, and feigning horror.

"My friends and I didn't bother to go over, but we heard, later, that he had a shriveled finger in the box, and claimed that it was a magic charm. I really didn't believe that story—until now. At the time, I thought it was just a dumb trick.

"The more I think of Principal Matthews and that creep Hoover, I remember that is was those kids who they seemed to seek them out at rather odd times and places: Back behind the bleachers after school, or in a far corner of the gymnasium. A few of them, I noted their names, even owned up to the fact that Hoover provided them with the avenue to obtain cocaine. None of the kids I spoke to even missed Matthews. But none of them like the Vice-Principal, Martin, at all.

"Word was that you could also score cocaine from the goths at a fairly easy cost. Some of the kids would seek them out before a weekend party. But the drug thing was fairly restricted to certain groups of kids who seemed to work through Hoover. The jocks and cheerleaders seemed remarkably clean, it was the fringe groups that seemed to have corner on the market."

"Justine, did you see any types of symbols or tattoos on those kids?"

"Now that you mention that, BJ, there was something with circles and a cross, probably several different colors. I saw some of those on one jacket and a similar tattoo on a few of the guys. They were usually kids on the 'fringe' who also had an in on the available drugs. Many of the kids believed that Hoover was the master contact."

"What about the three most recent victims: Ruth, Annette, and Vincent; where—if anywhere—do they fit into this mix. They all had those tattoos!"

"Well, BJ, like you know, they weren't a part of any special crowd, at least not Ruth and Annette. You know that I had some contact – on and off—with both girls. Not being jocks, artists, or cheerleaders—they were pretty typical of many of these students trying to find a place to fit in. Now that I think of it, they once talked about some special "mystery-history' kinda club that met off campus. And I think they spoke to Vincent, the senior, about somehow getting involved. The kids who are in the 'out crowd' truly seek their outlets in some non-school activities.

"They even invited me to a meeting. They meet in the parking lot/grounds of the Cowtown Rodeo. Some of the kids had even stranger stories of the club.

They spoke of some weird sexual elements and requirements to join the cult. But they never were explicit."

BJ interrupted Justine in mid-sentence. BJ had just heard about Cowtown from Vincent's parents. He had done some preliminary research after Jade teased him for not knowing about it. Cowtown billed itself as the oldest weekly rodeo in the USA. The rodeo had been operating since 1929 in the town of Pilesgrove, next to the Delaware River near the bridge from Delaware to New Jersey. He hadn't been there, but locals frequently made the roughly one-hour drive down for some western style fun and take in the huge flea market that was alongside the Rodeo parking lot!

"Tell me more about this mystery-history club meeting and the rodeo, that sounds like something fairly interesting."

"BJ, it might sound interesting, but to hear the students talk about it—there was a fairly sinister tone. You met in the parking lot of the Rodeo where their leaders asked them to step into several vans. Some kids said that 'bags' were put over their head as they drove to a secret portion of the Pine Barrens. They talked, rather cautiously, of 'special membership' and 'initiation rites'. The leaders were not from our school. They appeared to be somewhat older— maybe college age. They spoke about a small group of leaders who were not from this school. I don't know how much of this is true or whatever."

Justine continued, "When I pursued this discussion, none of the students actually mentioned attending, they were just referencing some friends who attended. Including Vincent, Ruth, and Annette."

"Justine, maybe we can explore a way get to one of those meetings. That would really give us some further insights..." said BJ.

At this point, Jade exploded, "That's about enough, BJ, I've let her be a 'junior detective' but this could be getting too dangerous at this point."

"Just a thought—I withdraw the request!" said BJ.

"Wait a minute, it does sounded rather interesting to me," suggested Justine.

Jade just sat and bristled. BJ tried to change the subject, "I wonder if the Professor can give us some additional clarity, particularly on the symbols and ritualistic stuff you, Todd, found in the clearing? We need to get back with him! If anybody knows about the mysterious stuff of these Pines it is sure him!"

Pine-Bog Annie just sat to the side watching and listening all of this with a sad face. Searching into her cup of black coffee and whimpered… "My poor Kelly". This situation was extending far beyond 'poor Kelly'. There were as many as seven deaths that they knew of within the past several months—and no one, as of yet, had connected them. Mainly because none of the victims were particularly special or of notice. That is until the rather prominent incident involving Matthews and Hoover.

Before they left, Jade pulled BJ close and whispered, "I'm getting even more worried now. We've brought Justine into the picture. You better take care of yourself and her! You're a teacher, not a cop; let Collins handle this now."

"Sorry Jade, I'll work closely with Collins but I am hooked into this, I have to see it through. I'll take care of Justine. Don't forget, you're the one who introduced me to Pine-Bog Annie!"

Collins heard this and suggested that it was time for BJ to consider carrying a weapon for protection. He also assured Jade that he would be looking out for Justine as well.

BJ: "I never shot a gun, never carried one."

"I have an extra revolver. I suggest you let me teach you how to use it and keep it with you if you do any more exploring!" He went to his car, brought in a small handgun and took BJ upstairs to show him the rudiments of carrying and using.

Jade interrupted them, "Don't forget, the Professor wants to meet with me and Justine. I need to make an appointment."

"Sure, but Collins and I should come along with you, I think he can help us wrap our heads around this problem."

Jade gave him a tight hug and a warm kiss. Justine said goodnight. Annie was gone for the evening. Collins walked BJ to his car.

"I think we finally have the department aware of the problem. I'll stay close to developments on my end, and you can continue to work the school and the kids. Just stay safe and keep that gun close to you."

Chapter 23
The Lent – 7 March–23 April 2000

Lent has always been a traditional commemoration to Jesus who spent 40 days in the desert. The historic Council of Nicea established this practice in 325 Ad. Traditionally, the 40 days do not include Sunday, therefore it tends to vary slightly every year. In 2000, Lent ran from 7 March through 23 April.

BJ continued to feel overwhelmed with the convergence of events in his life: ex-wife, baseball practice (his opening game was in another few weeks!), teaching responsibilities, his relationship with Jade, and his attempts to re-connect with his own children. But his major focus is drawn to the events that are pulling him further and further into a strange and somewhat mystical series of events he had never expected to face!

Even before Fat Tuesday, BJ had observed that his single work to help Pine-Bog Annie find her daughter had now exploded into a number of critical areas. The stage now seemed to be set for a final act.

BJ had completed the interviews with the three parents from the murdered school students. The information that he garnered, supported by Justine's work at the school reinforced his belief that some sort of cult was at the center of these murders. This was further strengthened once BJ had interviewed the owner of the tattoo parlor.

BJ took increasing personal heat for his relationship with Principal Matthews up until that fateful night at the restaurant. But this did not particularly surprise BJ. From New Year's Eve until his disappearance, BJ had witnessed the deterioration of Clarke Matthews—both the Principal and the man.

As the faculty and student body raised more and more concerns, he became bitterly defensive and openly angry—particularly at faculty meetings. He shouted down any opposition. The teachers were either strongly frightened or pissed with his behavior. He was clearly a man on the verge of a mental breakdown—if he wasn't there already. But was he really gone?

In the absence of the Principal, "Doc" Martin temporarily assumed the reins at the school but even his quiet and solid demeanor couldn't stem the flood of discontent that was beginning to surface from both the faculty and student body. BJ found himself in the middle a volatile school situation, but was obtaining help from Jade's daughter, Justine, who was a current senior.

The drug piece of the mystery was now emerging with some clarity. The school administration was certainly a party to the distribution. But how did that relate to these cults?

And BJ had just uncovered, with the help of Jade, what seemed to be a pattern of ritualistic murders that he was able to trace back to events in South Jersey during Lent in 1987, 1993, and now, 2000! But this didn't even explain Kelly's death.

BJ was soon to meet again with the Professor. When not teaching and preparing for baseball season, BJ had been spending much of this time on his research. He mailed those to the Professor for his review and opinion. He was brimming with confidence and anxious anticipation, as he got closer to the meeting. BJ hoped to establish a direct contact with this seeming cult of hereto unidentified people living in the Pines.

Chapter 24
Another Black Pieter Visit – 1 April 2000

Surprisingly, Santes invited them to meet with him the afternoon of Palm Sunday. This made it easier for BJ to put his full team together. Jade had to get coverage for the bar, but Collins and Justine were both available. Since the death of Hoover and the absence of Matthews, his superior officers were giving Collins more 'free reign' in the case. They were finally getting to visit the Professor. Todd agreed to meet them at the Professor's cabin.

BJ prepped the women for what was about to occur. "Just sit back and let him ask the questions, I need to press him for what he has discovered in his neck of these woods. I am just a little curious why he wanted to meet both of you."

They saw Collins' car in the driveway as they pulled up to the cabin. As they pulled down the dirt road and up to the cabin, the Professor was sitting comfortably in the rocker on his porch alongside Collins. He raised his tall frame as they emerged from the car. Todd stood up as well.

"So glad that you could all make it today! I have heard much about you from BJ and wanted to see you both for myself." He warmly hugged both of them. BJ had remembered to bring some extra donuts for Santes to put out with his tea. "Ah, so I see you knew about Fat Tuesday, I've been sacrificing throughout Lent and am looking forward to the Easter release. Please join me, come into the cabin, I have made some tea for you—we can share the donuts!

"BJ, you didn't tell me about your knowledge of the Lenten season. It was always a rich part of my Caribbean heritage. You know I was raised, as a young man, in North Jersey, but I was born in Jamaica. That led to my fascination with the culture of that area.

"As you asked me, BJ, I have been looking into some of the youth groups that have formed in the depths of these Pines. Most are loosely connected to some of the churches that I have been speaking with. Most of these churches are 'non-denominational', which means they are not affiliated with any larger group. But many of those in this area are loosely connected with the Roman Catholic faith.

"I asked Jade and Justine here for two reasons. One reason is that I have already mentioned: I just wanted to meet the interesting and pretty girls that BJ has been speaking to me about. The second reason is to ask you more about Pine-Bog Annie and her daughter, Kelly.

"When you first came to see me, it focused on Annie and Kelly. But now the circle seems to have widened. You filled me in on the three high school students, and I have now read of the death and disappearance of the high school Principal and death of a teacher. I, like BJ, am trying to make some sense and connection out of these events. BJ asked me to do some investigation down here, and I did it, primarily through my church contacts. The young people are pretty open with me, I told BJ that they refer to me as 'Black Pieter' and I don't really try to correct them."

Professor Santes began to question the women:

"Jade, what more can you tell me about Pine-Bog Annie and Justine, did you know Kelly at all?"

Jade slowly and passionately repeated the story that they received from Annie and the subsequent information they had discovered.

"Justine, I know you weren't close with Kelly, but did she seem to have any connection with those young people you were observing in the school cafeteria. Did either of them know the Principal of the high school?"

Jade interrupted, "We can't seem to identify any relationship between either Kelly or Annie. There was some rumors—unconfirmed, however, that the Principal had been a client of Kelly at some point."

Justine then proceeded to tell the Professor of the 'mystery-history' club and the alleged mysterious meeting in the depths of the Pines. The Professor's eyebrows raised at the mention of such a club.

BJ then added his investigation that took him to the tattoo parlor in Wildwood. He pushed the Professor to talk more about some of the mysterious activities that had infiltrated deep into these Pines. All the cards were now on the table. The ball was clearly in the professor's court.

The Professor paused thoughtfully. Then began to speak again.

"I contacted several of these small groups of friends that I identified through my church group made up primarily of older women. They were pretty open and shared some of their interesting beliefs. This has translated to some rather strange patterns within one or two of these small groups.

"I started investigating my roots while I was in college. It is interesting that my last name, Santes, is a variation from a strain of the Roman Catholic religion that developed in the Islands. 'Santerians' means 'Way of the Saints'; it is a combination of Yoruba (African tribe) mixed with Catholicism. Not unlike the Rastafarians this grew out of the initial slave trade in the Caribbean. It is a mix of formal religion and ancient tribal rituals.

"When I met with the young people down here, they seemed to have some rather corrupted Christian practices in place, a few of them still attend their local churches, but they do seem drawn to some rather mystical areas that remind me of the some of the Santerian sects I had read about. Many of the people who have migrated into New Orleans demonstrate what I would call 'corrupted Christianity'.

"The entire practice of the Voodoo came to New Orleans through the slave trade in the early 1700s. It was a sensationalized version of an earlier African religion. People today associate voodoo with zombies and the undead, but the original practice was much closer to Catholicism than anything else.

"I did notice some of those symbols that BJ asked me about, you know, the tricolored circles with the cross in the center. None of those emanate from the Voodoo practices, but they could be variations. The colors are significant. They focus on some naturalistic patterns: Blue—for the sky, Green for the earth, and Red for blood or death.

"I did some further research, and there is some evidence that there might be some element of 'sacrifice' in their practices. Some of these can be traced back to the Native Americans who initially inhabited this area. This was usually limited to animals, but it could be related to some of the dismemberments that have been uncovered."

"Professor, where do we go from here? What do you suggest?"

"Well, BJ, I might be able to have you meet with one of these groups if you think that could be helpful."

"Helpful! It could be very dangerous," said Jade. Justine nodded in agreement.

"These are my friends, ladies, they may be a bit odd and offbeat, but BJ will be very safe with me. In addition, it might be edifying for BJ to meet some true Pineys who are becoming acclimated to the rest of the world. You must know that the Amish living in Lancaster are facing similar challenges.

"The young men are not sure how to meet the challenges of the modern world. Their parents give them one year 'in the world' to see if they want to leave. Also, there has been an up-tick in the use of drugs among the Amish. I suspect that is true here as well. BJ and I will further the investigation!

"This raises another possibility. Among the Amish existed a group of people dating back to colonial America called the 'Shakers'. They were a highly charismatic faith, not unlike some versions of the Rastafarians, who actually began trembling during their services. But the oddest part of the religion was their celibacy. Procreation was forbidden after you joined, but they took in orphans and homeless. Needless to say, the religion died itself out.

"Even though our cult group seems rather modern and drug-connected, I wouldn't be surprised that you will find that they are perhaps 'too' conservative when it comes to sexual activity. You may be able to bring that out when we meet with them."

Jade and Justine were not convinced, but BJ felt comfortable enough to plan a date with Black Pieter to go and visit a few of these groups. Todd sat quietly, taking this all in. As they climbed back into BJ's van, they shared mixed emotions. Justine thought the Professor was really 'cool', but Jade still had some suspicions about his motivation. "Why is he doing all of this?"

"He and I hit it off after our very first meeting. He seems to be a sincere historian with a deep interest in this part of the state…and the relationship between Pineys and the Caribbean influence."

BJ continued, "If he knows these kids, as he says he does, maybe he know about this 'mystery-history' stuff? Something really strange is going on in these Pines and I just really believe he will get us even closer to the real truth!"

Just before the cars pulled away, BJ asked the professor if he could have a few last words. He signaled to his team to wait for a bit, and walked to the side of the porch with Peter. "Professor, I didn't want to get too creepy in there, but what about these missing body parts, particularly the ring fingers. And how does this play into Justine's story about Cowtown, Shakers, Pineys, and runaway slaves?"

The Professor replied, "Trust me, my friend, together we will seek the answer to all of your questions."

The remaining drive back to Staley's was reasonably quiet. At one point BJ's phone rang, but when he saw it was Cassie's exchange, he hung up before a message began. Jade didn't need to hear her at this point. Justine sat playing with her cell phone in the backseat. Jade sat quietly next to BJ, with only an occasional word of warning to the man she was thought she was growing to love.

Chapter 25
Children of Abraham –
Holy Wednesday, 2000

As Holy Week moved into gear, South Jersey was hit with another late show storm. It was a surprisingly cold and frosty day in an old frame house hidden somewhere deep in the Pine Barrens. It was now Holy Wednesday, a time when many churches celebrate Jesus washing the feet of his apostles. In this house gather another group of strange apostles!

A group of five people of rather indeterminate age are standing around a wood-burning stove. The house is not real modern, but it's also not ancient. It would be a real nice house if a mother was there to do the picking up and general cleaning. But at this point, it appears to be clearly teen-disheveled, soda and beer cans are strewn around the living area. Half-empty bags of chips and fast food are littered in the area. Ashtrays are filled with remnants of butts.

The group appeared to be involved in a ritualistic ceremony of some sort. They are referencing the Santerians. They begin to discuss the *Ring of Sixes*, and the need for some sort of sacrifices, with an invocation to some unnamed spirits. It appears that this is one of those offshoots of the Caribbean religions, although it is unclear to the nature of this odd group.

The obvious leader was an ebony-black female with short-cropped hair, strong-muscular arms. She was very tall. Her tall posture and poise makes her stand out as the leader of this crew. Looking closely, you could see a sixth finger on her left hand. Many people consider the sixth finger more of a myth than a reality.

But, truth be told, close family relational marriages often produce this 'birth defect' in the Pinelands. Most people today have the finger surgically removed to avoid the attention, but this strong woman seemed to flaunt it!

No one really knew her background. She was a college graduate with her roots among the historical former slaves who inhabited these Pines. She had abandoned her Catholic Faith while in college and found solace in the spiritual practices of the Caribbean that she had visited in her earlier youth.

Sitting next to her was a rather plain, pale-skinned, female with bright blue eyes. Unlike the leader, this frail girl had been the victim of sexual abuse as a young girl. This trauma led her to seek out a new form of faith.

She is sitting next to a young, apparently, albino man. He is also a long-time resident of the Pines. His parents were descended from the Jackson Whites who had migrated here in the late 1700s. He had inherited the Albino gene that set him so far apart from his classmates while he was in high school. He dropped out and found that the "Abraham Faith" was much more to his satisfaction.

The remaining two people are 'Sonny and Cher' lookalikes. He was fairly short with a thick broad forehead, signs of early baldness. He has the tricolored tattoo on his right arm with the cross in the middle. Next to him is a white, punker type, blatantly sexual by her clothing and make-up and clinging to him. They had been a couple in high school and moved together into the cult because it allowed them to remain together in an unusual relationship.

All five of them are missing the ring finger on their left hand!

Overhearing their conversations, you realize that none of these people are current students. They speak of activities that indicate they have some other means of employment. "Grace" works in one of the clubs in AC. "Sonny" and "Cher" apparently work at a few of the stands on the Wildwood Boardwalk. The Albino and the pale girl both work for some cleaning service based in Cape May. They all seem to have enough means to maintain this home in the pines. There are three major bedrooms located off the main room that now serves as the chapel: for their service.

There is a strange-shaped alter at the front of the room which resembles a coffin. The leader steps to the center and begins to quietly chant in a strange language. The group begins to circle around her, joining hands. They begin to join in prayers that sound vaguely like those you would hear at a Catholic Mass. The leader begins to ask the remainder of the group to offer up prayer requests. "Grace" begins by praying to Father Abraham. The others all kneel at the name.

"Father Abraham, hear our prayer. As we approach the Easter season, we seek you help as we gather our sacrifices for your purpose. Aid us in our actions. Aid us in our search for more to bring to you. We pray that you will make us successful be with each one of our small groups as we move to the completion of your goals for us."

Father Abraham was a reference to the patriarch of both the Jewish and Muslim faith. Abraham, of Genesis fame, was chosen by God to lead a great people. He didn't have a son with his wife until they were both over 90! When his son, who he waited for all those years, was about 16, God told Abraham to take his son, Isaac (in the Jewish tradition) to the top of a mountain and to kill him there.

This is one of the most difficult passages in the entire bible. How could a father ever kill his own son? God intervenes and Isaac is saved! But this stark image of a man preparing to murder his own son has haunted both Christian and Jews over the centuries.

We also understand that ritualistic sacrifice has been a part of many cultures throughout the history of the world. Several older cultures, with rich roots to their ancient past, still engage in the execution of children.

But these people are now in the new millennium! One would think they would be different. But even in modern cultures, we sacrifice the children in the womb for reasons of comfort. Or, as in China, female fetuses are aborted after detection of their sex through ultra sound. Is it therefore, surprising that this young cult holds a different value on human life? Yet, part of their ritual focuses on abstinence from sex and marriage. Much like the 'Shakers' of old, this small clan clings to a concept that values life in a far different way.

As the prayers conclude, they all begin to speak. One can overhear the invocation of the names: one by one—Gleeson, Jade, Justine, Annie, Matthews, Hoover and other names that no one would recognize. They appear to be lifting up these names to some higher power.

There is a pause in the ceremony. The woman leader asks, "What are those people trying to find out? Who is that teacher from the high school? Are they on to us?"

"Mistress," replies the pale young woman standing next to him, "Gleeson and his girlfriend are just trying to help Pine-Bog Annie, and we all know that Kelly was her daughter."

"Bullshit," she says, "they are getting too close to us...we need to be careful. Kelly was an accident. Some of our group took her out of season. We let our anger overtake our proper procedures.

"For now, we need to curtail our 'rides' from the Cowtown Rodeo. They seem to be getting too much attention."

The others all remark on Justine. They are aware that she has been looking into their activities. Then turn their attention to a discussion of Matthews. "Do we know where that Principal, Matthews, has gone to?" said one of the group.

The tall black woman steps forward. "He has been sighted in these Pines since his disappearance but not lately. We have a mark on him. Perhaps he has come under the influence of Father Abraham? Easter is fast approaching and we must complete our cycle of life by then."

"Patience, brothers and sisters," pleads the leader, "we will still have time for a complete ceremony prior to Easter. We must rid ourselves of these distractions."

They ramble on for a bit before settling into what amounts to be the end of the ceremony. They finish the meeting with something resembling a communion service with the leader distributing a substance in a cup to each of the remaining four participants. They are all on their knees surrounding the leader, the stove, and the "communion material". They appear to be reciting a quiet yet elaborate chant as they partake in the "meal" that is offered. The contexts of the prayer requests are unclear, particularly to the figure standing outside the window of the cabin. The group is totally unaware of the presence.

The figure has been standing in the shadow of the trees near the cabin, quietly observing and listening. As he strides back through the woods, he reminisces about his trips back to the islands over the years. He thinks about the many rituals that he has observed. He chuckles to himself and wonders what this crew would think if they knew that he was there!

Chapter 26
BJ Visits the Cult – Holy Thursday, 2000

BJ was never good at waiting, and time seemed to stand still waiting for the Professor to arrange the meeting. The day has finally arrived for Peter and BJ to make the visit with what may be a key youth cult group from the region. There had been several broken engagements, mainly related to the group. It was now Holy Thursday, just a few days before Easter. Peter has made the arrangements, but asks to meet with BJ at his cabin prior to leaving. As BJ makes the ride into the Pines, he finally decides to call back Cassie. He had not returned her call. She answered on the second ring!

"I thought you were never getting back to me. I am concerned."

"What's the problem, Cassie, I thought you were getting reasonably positive over my reconnection with James and Carly?"

"Yes, but Carly filled me in on your 'investigative activities' that you are trying to involve her in."

"Wait, no, she offered to help, I didn't respond. This problem is my problem! I need to work it out. It involves my job, my new friends, and an increasing web of deep issues affecting many people and families!"

"Oh, I'm sorry if I overreacted, but when Carly talked about you bringing body parts to her lab, I—"

"Cassie, don't worry, that was her idea, not mine. We are developing a good bond right now, work with us, not against us."

"OK, BJ, thanks for the clarification, I just freaked out over comments about the body parts. Stay safe." Cassie hung up.

BJ was still trying to make sense of the conversation as he pulled up to the Professor's cabin.

On his arrival, the Professor shares his concerns with BJ. "I quietly went down to their cabin a few days ago. I'm not quite sure what we are going to find if and when we speak with them."

Peter briefly describes the students that he saw. These seem to somewhat resemble the group that Jade and he had seen in the Delaware mall. BJ was still game to meeting this group in order to shed some light on the developing incidents. The Professor now seems somewhat reluctant to pursue the meeting on this day. But he seemed to give in to BJ and proceeded to establish a meeting place with the group at a diner on Route 50, close to the Pine Barrens. At the same time, though, Santes is suggesting that BJ considers pulling the plug on his investigation.

"BJ, I've grown fond of you. I am beginning to worry about this obsession that you seem to have over Annie and Kelly. She's gone and Annie is improving, why don't you let it go?"

"Peter, it's not just Kelly, you know what's going on, this is reaching out to other young people in this region. It has even impacted the staff at the school. I think I've told you about this strange seven-year pattern in this area. You are a true historian, doesn't this beg our investigation?"

"I'm just worried about you. I can tell that Jade and you are building a great relationship and I don't want this to pull you away from her."

"Professor, I owe this, to both Jade and Annie." BJ pressed on. "Annie keeps thinking Kelly's death was just a result of her prostitution. If there was a broader and wider explanation, she needs to know this to bring closure to her mourning."

Reluctantly, Peter picks up his phone and makes a call. "We're ready to meet you now, and are your people still ready to talk with my friend?" Peter is quiet, and then says, "OK, meet you in 30 minutes."

When they pull into the parking lot, they see 5 people standing near a van in the back of the parking lot. Two young women, two young men, and a tall black woman who led them are walking toward BJ and his group.

"Black Peter, this the guy who wants to talk with us?" It was a tall, striking black woman who spoke. She was dressed totally in black and wearing four-inch spike-heeled boots. She imbued both sexuality and power simultaneously. She appeared to be the leader of the group.

"You agreed to meet with us," said the professor.

"Now that I see him, I'm not so sure. Maybe we can just meet out here without going inside."

"Look, I'm not a cop, I'm just trying to find out what's been going on at the high school and what happened to a friend's daughter," added BJ.

One of the other guys with them said, "Ain't you the baseball coach at school—loser."

"Yes, and I teach in the history department. I don't recognize any of you. Did any of you attend Central Pines?"

"All of us have either graduated or dropped out and a couple of our newer members are still in that 'jail' you call a school. We still have a lot of friends in that place," said the pale blond girl.

"Get on with your questions, for the sake of this old black dude," said the black woman, motioning to the Professor.

"Let me risk 'pissing' all of you off," challenged BJ. "Did you guys know that the Principal and his buddy, Hoover, were fencing cocaine at the school? Was the mob closing in on any of you?

"Man, are you pushing it, or what...cocaine flowed like baby powder at that school while Matthews and Hoover were there. Dried up now!" said the Grace Jones lookalike leader. "But we never seen any gangster types around the school, just those two creeps. They managed the flow."

BJ continued to press the issue: "What about those other kids who ended up dead, was that due to Matthews and Hoover. And by the way, have any of you heard anything from Matthews since Hoover was found dead?"

They became suddenly very quiet, then the leader continued: "Boy, are you ever nosy! We have no idea what happened to those other kids, they weren't a part of our select club. As far as Matthews, word is that he is in hiding somewhere, possibly in the Pines. We'd love to find him!"

BJ interrupted him, "I am just worried about what is happening in that school and in these Pines... And I'm not ready to give up figuring out what happened to my friend's daughter. And I guess I'm curious, as a history teacher, about this special club you guys are involved with—mystery-history something. I know that you pick kids up at the local Rodeo, blindfold them, and take them somewhere into the Pines! What's with that anyway?"

Grace spoke again: "Now you are getting too close and personal! We have developed a very quiet and private 'religion', if you will, down in these parts.

We don't force anyone to join, because we can be rather demanding. We are not some 'hippy-dippy' cult that you heard about in the 60s.

"We have some rather serious beliefs that we prefer to keep to a small group of believers. Yes, we blindfold the new potential converts; that way, if they don't like what we offer, we can just drop them back at the Rodeo and end the relationship. And yes, we do use some mild drugs in our practices, but you would be very surprised to find out how very pure we really are! So, we don't think we can really help you. If we ever find Matthews, we will let the Professor know.

"As a matter of fact, we have some business to take care of tonight for the upcoming events leading up to Easter," she said. With this the she turned, motioned to her entourage, and they began to move back toward the van that had brought them to the diner.

They peeled out of the gravel driveway, but as they left, some papers trailed out of the back window of their van. BJ bent down to pick them up. He was disturbed at what he read. There was a current heavy metal band named Slayer. What BJ picked up were some of the lyrics that drifted out of the departing van. "Angel of Death", "Raising Blood", "God Hates us All"; laced with sayings like "surgery without anesthesia", "Feel the Knife Pierce your Intestines…"

He showed these to Peter who simply shrugged his shoulders. "I don't know what is going on with that group, but in spite of what you just saw and read, I don't think they are anything but just a group of Pineys trying to figure out the world—just like those Amish boys in Lancaster."

"They sure seem dangerous to me."

"BJ, let me work with them, you just continue your other work, and I'll let you know if I uncover anything else. Let's go home now. This is getting us nowhere."

BJ climbed behind the wheel, the Professor slowly got in beside him and they drove, silently, back to Peter's cabin in the woods.

BJ dropped the professor off and headed back to Staley's to reconnect with Jade and Collins who were waiting for him. He was deeply disturbed with what he had seen. He was also somewhat concerned that the Professor was rather nonchalant about the situation and was indirectly asking BJ to step back.

Was this just an odd group of heavy metal Goths from the Pines, or were they capable of what the "Slayer" lyrics suggested. How did this group in the

Pines go this far astray? And what about Matthews, they indicated that he might still be in the Pines—and they were looking for him. Also, these people weren't even old enough 7 or 14 years ago when these other murders happened.

He slumped into a chair in Jade's apartment; Justine and Collins had both been waiting for him along with Jade. Jade started, "What happened, you look shaken."

He was. BJ began to recount the events of the late afternoon. Jade agreed that the description of the group resembled to some extent, the kids they encountered at the Mall. But the group that BJ met was somewhat older. This strange, crude group didn't seem to fit the pattern of murders that had been occurring over the years and throughout all of South Jersey.

Collins spoke up, "If this group had anything to do with this, and I doubt it, then there had to be a mastermind behind their actions. They just don't seem that clever. And we still don't have a clue about Matthews and his disappearance made up to appear like to a mob hit. Could Matthews still be quietly behind all of this?"

BJ was dejected. "There is just not much more that we can do just now. I better leave this to the police, particularly now that they are involved with the Matthews-Hoover case."

Collins said goodnight and headed back out into the night. Jade and BJ sat almost staring across the room from each other. Finally, Jade took the first step and walked to the couch where BJ had been stationed. She sat next to him, grabbed his hand, and stared intently into his eyes.

"BJ, I'm deathly worried for you, but you have come too far to simply drop your efforts. Right now all I care about is you and me…and of course, Justine."

They both almost uttered the 'L' word, but instead shared a long and passionate kiss. BJ extricated himself from their embrace, said good-bye and headed back to Sea Isle and more reflection on both the murders and his relationship.

Later that same evening, two young teens pulled in with an old camper into a vacant site on Lake Mummie. They borrowed the parents' camper while their parents were on a weekend splurge in Atlantic City. They carefully find a spot under the trees to park the camper. The boy is careful not to scratch his dad's vehicle. But this is just too good a chance to miss!

This is to be a test of "first love". The couple talk, they pet, music plays on their cassette box. The boy unwraps what appears to be cocaine and they both indulge in the product. That gives them the urge to continue their experience. They soon reach the tipping point and he clumsily reached to undo the buttons on her blouse. She leans back and encourages him. He's not good at this, and he fumbles so badly that she undoes them for him, giggling lovingly at his ineptness.

They are too engrossed in one another to pay attention to the quiet noise of a vehicle that has pulled into their clearing. They were too engrossed to the sound of soft footsteps as a quiet group moves into the area.

A tall black woman is leading her "troops" to the camper. She is making hand gestures and sounds of silence as she directs the four others. Suddenly, they burst into action. The two young men with the group knock on the door of the camper. The couple jumps up, initially fearful that their parents have found them. But seeing the knives brandished by the two young men, they quickly become fearful for their lives.

"Take whatever you want!" the boy partially screams. The girl is just whimpering slowly as she tries to put her blouse back on. "We have a little money, it's all yours, just leave us alone!"

The black woman enters the cabin. "We don't want or need your money, but Father Abraham needs you."

"Who is Father Abraham?"

"Just come outside, quietly, and you will find out for yourselves."

Quietly, hoping that everything will be all right, the couple gets up and exits the camper. They notice that the two young men have moved to the gathering of scattered wood in the area, while two girls are quietly chanting: "For you, Father Abraham... For you..."

They watch as the men begin to pile the wood in the center of the clearing, while the girls continue their prayerful chant. The leader stands quietly and stares at them. The young couple is frozen with fear in their own footprints.

One of the boys lights a fire. A large two-part stake, resembling a cross, has been placed in the center of the beginning conflagration.

The leader asks the couple to place their hands on the hood of the camper. The two boys move from the fire to hold each one in place. She takes a long knife from her belt and swiftly, almost surgically, severs the right ring finger on each. She does this so quickly they almost cannot react. But as the blood begins to squirt over the van, the boy begins to scream and the girl passes out in the arms of her captive. The two girls each move forward and pick up the fingers and put them in two small leather boxes.

Both the boy and girl are dragged to the rim of the fire. Both are fastened to the roughhewn cross that has been set to the side. They are tied to the wood as the two boys lift them up and place them at the edge of the fire. All of them help to push the burning wood under the cross until the clothes of the two begin to catch fire.

The girl has regained consciousness and begins to scream in concert with the boy who never lost consciousness. The screams are brief, however, since the super heat of the fire has reached their lungs—they are gone!

But the five are not! They continue to chant:

"We have sacrificed for you, Father Abraham.

"We have drawn blood for you, Father Abraham.

"We have kept remembrances for you, Father Abraham.

"Bless us, Father Abraham."

As the fire ebbs, the charred remains are carefully collected, wrapped and placed in the back of their car. The team leaves the clearing by using a portable leaf blower to destroy their footprints. The crew backs out of the area and enter their van parked at the side of the clearing. They seem very pleased with themselves.

As they slowly pull away, in the shadow of the pines stands a tall figure in a dark coat, nodding approval.

Chapter 27
Good Friday Visit – 21 April 2000

BJ is becoming frustrated with the seeming lack of any solution to the problems. The "balls in the air" are still floating and BJ is waiting for them to descend so he can catch some of them, at least. School is about to be dismissed for the Easter break. The team meets on the evening of Maundy Thursday (20 April 2000) to discuss the events of the last month.

BJ is behaving like the team leader, "coach" that he was. He was still too much of a teacher. He was coming to believe that they were just placating his desire to be a detective. But they all came into Jade's tavern and sat down at a corner table.

BJ began, "Let's see what we can piece together and then set up a plan for our next steps… Todd, what is the latest word from the law enforcement end?"

"I have several items to share. To begin with, we had another notice of two young people who were reported to have gone missing from Woodbine." Both parents had come to the station where Todd was located. He sat and spoke with them.

"To be honest," said one of the fathers, "these kids have been seeing each other for a while. I suspected that they might have just kinda eloped."

"But," said one of the wives, "with this nonsense in the paper about murders, we just thought we would bring it to you." Todd took copious notes, listened attentively and told them that it was very early in the "missing stage" but he would put this out as an alert to the rest of the State.

"In addition, there was a report of a fire in the Camp Mummie campgrounds. Our troopers investigated and found a similar situation to the one we found several months ago off the Garden State Parkway. No signs of bodies, but blood and evidence of a fire made of wood from the area. Once again, there were no signs of footprints at the scene. These two stories could very well be connected based on what we have been uncovering."

"Is this getting some major attention from the FBI or other higher authorities?"

"The Feds, at this point, seem more focused on the accident we uncovered. There efforts are concentrated on the drug action and cartels that appear to be operating out of Atlantic City. Our barracks commander has reached out to them, but to this point it appears that we are not important enough here in the Pines! This is still being addressed as simply runaway kids.

"No one is putting two and two together like we are! Our troopers now on high alert because of what they have personally seen. It may not mean much to the local papers or FBI, but it is sure scaring the hell out of them."

"What about Principal Matthews, any sightings?"

Jade interjected, "I heard Justine say they thought some kids had seen him around—in the woods—but I don't know how valid that might be. That seems rather unlikely!"

"We are still talking to folks at the school, but no real evidence or indications from them," added Collins. "He had no family in this area that we know of. His parents are both dead and his ex-wife lives in California."

"What about the Columbian Cartel? Any presence in this area or Atlantic City?"

"Well, the Feds are following up on that. But, for now, they don't appear to be active outside of Atlantic City, although those may have been Columbians that took Matthews and Hoover from the restaurant. But I doubt that they are from this area at all. It is possible that they simply took Matthews and dumped him somewhere else after they got whatever information they wanted from him," added Collins.

"What about that 'cult gang' we saw in Delaware?" said Jade. "BJ said that, at first, but after meeting the other crew—they seemed decidedly older. Justine thought they sounded like a few of the kids from her school."

Collins continued, "We tried to identify a few of them from our juvenile records with no real success. Two or three of them are or were former students at Pinelands Regional. They were just plain C-students with no disciplinary records other than occasional truancy. Just like a lot of kids at Regional."

BJ nodded in the affirmative. "But I still think they may be involved in this to some degree, but not for 15 years. Keep in mind that we seem to have uncovered a seven-year pattern: 1986, 1993 and now 2000! That's between 7 and 14 years ago. They would have been infants or 10-year-olds. There is something beyond all of this that we are missing.

"Todd, what have you discovered about the Professor, he seemed like a real straight shooter, but he became a little uncomfortable when we went to approach the cult gang. I don't know if he was just scared, or what."

"I did some homework on him, in our preliminary research he comes up squeaky clean. Fine career at Rutgers, retires to part-time work down here, moves into the Pines, and works closely with the area aged and church groups. Sounds like a grown-up boy scout. But there are still a few gaps on his 'resume' that have me still searching—to be on the safe side.

"But we really need to focus on this cult group that the Professor took me to see. It's a bit odd that he has come to know them. They are indeed a strange crew."

BJ continued to share his experiences with the odd group. They were all attentive as he took them through his visit.

"They were, in one sense, reluctant to talk to me," continued BJ. "But on the other hand, they were almost bragging about their practices. They even defended putting a sack over people's heads to protect their 'group'. To be honest, they scared me. It wasn't the size of the group, or the strength of their members, but there was a sinister quality about them that disturbed me."

They sit and commiserate with one another. BJ had convinced Jade to join him at the local Catholic church for the Maundy Thursday communion service. BJ was not used to the Catholic observance of communion—the heavy references to the actual body and blood reminded him of what was transpiring within the Pine Barrens. He kept his thoughts to himself and enjoyed the solemn beauty of the service.

Another concern creeped into BJ's mind. The service he had just participated in reminded him of the way that the Professor's discussion of Rastafarians and Santerians demonstrated their ability to twist and shape Christianity into their own model, the very way that some more accepted Christian denominations bend and vary their own beliefs and practices. But the twisting he saw with both of these historical and modern practices—combined to his meeting with the "five" screamed at his sensibilities.

The service left both Jade and BJ in a pensive mood at they reflected on their live and their new relationships. But this was silent stuff with just eye contact and sitting close... Collins was musing about his ex-wife and his current status at the state police barracks.

BJ continued to think about the family he had basically deserted—even though it was his wife who had kicked him out! He was equally frustrated that the murders—even though they were spread out—were not getting the attention they demanded. Justine just sat quietly, humming music, and playing on her cell phone. She kept her inner fears quiet enough.

Pretty soon the empty glasses and wine bottles indicate that they had been meeting long enough. They concluded that just BJ and Jade would make one more visit to the Professor. "He seemed more comfortable when Jade was around and maybe he can help us get a better read on the gang of five that we've seen. The practices of those five is disturbing, to say the least."

Collins warned BJ to bring the gun with him if he was going to meet that gang again, and further suggested that he would try to shake loose to join them if he could.

Collins departs, leaving Jade and BJ to one another. They moved upstairs to her apartment. Justine was going over to stay with a friend tonight, so they had some real private time to take advantage. First, however, BJ called the Professor to make an appointment with him for tomorrow during the day. He tells him that he will bring Jade along—and maybe Collins.

Peter seems a bit distracted by the request, but agrees to meet them at his cabin around noon. Jade took the telephone from BJ's hand and gently led him to her bedroom! They make quiet and gentle love well into the night.

When they arrived at their destination on Good Friday, around noon, the Professor was not quite his usual calm and poised self. He begins to reveal fears he has about too much contact with this group that that he fears could become dangerous.

"I'll have my friend tag along for extra help."

"No, just you and Jade and me should be fine, I'll be more relaxed by the time we meet them. Today is Good Friday and I am due at a special service at a local church at 2:00 PM.

"I think it's better to meet them on their turf. BJ, you are right, they may be at the heart of this, but I think—if we are careful—I can convince them to turn in their leader or leaders whomever they may be.

"I will call each of you in the morning."

As Jade and BJ drove back home, they discussed the Professor and the plan.

"If we stick together, and have Collins as backup, I really think we can pull this off. Although, Jade, I am concerned about involving you in this anymore. I deeply care about you and Justine and have increasing worries about dragging you into this."

"Oh BJ, I can handle myself, besides I will be with you and (eventually) Collins—and now that you even have a gun that you know how to use. I'm really not afraid of the old Professor; I think he'll take good care of me. I am confident in you. You have convinced me that you can handle this."

"Great, count on BJ, the gunslinger. I'm not sure how much protection I can offer, but you know I will always be there for you. I am starting to have some doubts about how much Peter can really help us. But I think we are very near to a solution.

"Jade, even though it's getting late, we need to talk—not at the beach— not at the bar, let's go to a very special, out of the way place—Captain Crabbe's."

Jade smiled, leaned over, and kissed BJ on the cheek. Jade had recommended Crabbe's to BJ when he first came down to this area. It was on an off the beaten path road just South of Atlantic City and west of Route 9 and the Parkway. A good bar, great seafood specials, and the hottest horseradish on the East Coast!

Not particularly romantic, but they could get a quiet booth in the corner. By now it was close to 9:00 PM and the supper crowd was down—due to the time and Good Friday. This was always a good opportunity to get Jade away from her own establishment.

They settled in with some drinks and a basket of blue-claw crabs. Jade ordered wine, but BJ needed a good pitcher of beer to wash down his crab!

"Jade, this is all coming to a head, and during Easter Week! I want to make sure we are both on the same page and moving in the same direction. I know you have some real concerns about Justine's involvement. You also know that I am having some issues as I try to reconnect with my kids—and I think that's bothering you somewhat." BJ was slowly breaking and cleaning the meat out of his crabs as he talked.

"BJ, I'm honestly not sure if you're over your first marriage yet. There is a real special bond forming between you and I. Neither of us uses the L word, even though we engage in it! I'm not sure where this is going, and I'm not sure if you even know which direction you are heading in."

"Jade, both of us are bringing our share of baggage into this relationship. You are rooted in your business. I am struggling mightily to see what direction I am heading into. I love this investigative stuff, but I'm no trained policeman.

"Sometimes I feel I am way over my head, yet on other occasions I'm convinced that I am way ahead of the state police on this situation. I'm a mess. But you have a way of making me feel so much better about myself. I don't want to lose that!"

"I hear you, BJ, and you do the same things for me. But is this for the long haul, or are we just a temporary holding station?"

"I want it to be more than that, but only time will tell. We both know that the next two to three days should show some results to all our efforts. We have a good team working and pulling for us. When this is behind us, we need to really take stock in our future. Where do we both want to be ten years from now—and what do we want to be doing."

"BJ, I can't think beyond tomorrow right now. Let's just enjoy one another while we have time like this together. For now, shut up, drink your beer, and finish your crab."

"Good advice."

They finished up and there was a long drive back to Jade's home in Belleplain, both were very quiet after the deep discussion they had shared. BJ dropped Jade off and headed back to his apartment. He was increasingly concerned with their relationship, but the next few days should bring all of his problems and concerns into focus.

Chapter 28
He Descended into Hell – 22 April 2000

BJ slept in on Saturday morning. A cool spring sun shone through his window to serve as his alarm clock. He staggered out to the kitchen for a coffee and then saw that he had left his phone on the chair in the living room. He saw that he had missed several calls, on from Jade, two from Carly and one from his son, James—but there was only one voicemail:

"BJ, I've headed down to the professor's cabin, you must have overslept. Don't worry though; I brought Justine along for company. The Professor had even mentioned that Justine just might be helpful with kids her own age. We'll meet you there. See you soon…"

BJ was more than a bit concerned that Jade brought Justine along, but Jade knew what she was doing. She had been reticent to involve Justine from the beginning. Maybe she was more comfortable with his plan now? He called Collins, but got his answering machine. He let him know the plan for the day. He dressed quickly, put his new weapon in his belt, and began to drive down towards the cabin.

As he drove, he reached out to James (again)—but he was not picking up. He then tried Carly, who did answer.

"Dad, glad you called. I heard you cleared Mom's mind about my strange request. But I am concerned about what is going on in South Jersey. I read the paper about your missing Principal and the deaths that have occurred at your school. I guess I'm worried about you."

"Thanks Carly, but I've got it under control. I'm working with a good amateur team assisted by a very competent State Trooper. I'm on my way down to one of my team member's home right now. Remember I told you about the Professor?"

"Yes, I do, well I just want you to know that I love you and look forward to your next visit, bye now!"

BJ smiled as he hung up and finished his journey to the Pines. *Things have a way of working out on a positive note*, he mused.

However, when he arrived at the Professor's home, he was surprised to find it empty. Jade's car was sitting in the driveway. The door was locked and no one answered. The lock appeared rather flimsy, but he was no lock-picker. He began to slowly panic. He called Collins again, and again got no answer.

He paced around the back of the property, still no sign of anyone and no opening. He looked through the windows and the cabin appeared to be empty. Becoming desperate, BJ picked up a large rock from the side garden and smashed out the nearest large window. He crawled in and opened the door. There was no sign of anyone. As he looked through the simple cabin, he saw what appeared to be a decorative feather sticking out from under the chair. BJ bent down and pulled out a long feathered earring; he recognized it as belonging to Jade. Now he really began to panic.

He called Collins for the third time. Still no answer, but this time he left a message for him to get down here as soon as possible. He then called Jade: no answer. He then headed outside to see where look for some signs of Jade or Justine. Hurriedly looking around, he finally saw what appeared to be large tracks from a van, that are heading out of this lot and turn into a dirt road just a few hundred feet from the Professor's cabin.

As his car bounced down a dirt road, BJ reached into his belt and pulled out his gun. He set it on the seat beside him, next to his cell phone. The track marks weave on that beaten down dirt road for about a mile and a half. BJ can't accelerate due to the condition of the path. He moves slowly over the path. He can't afford to crash and he also wants to be somewhat quiet. He has no idea what he is walking into.

He finally approaches a small clearing. He sees what appears to be an empty van parked about 100 yards from where he now stands where he sees the van parked. As he leaves the car and before he starts to move forward, he grabs his phone to call Collins again. Still busy, but he leaves another message.

He calls Jade, again, no answer. He walks slowly toward the van to investigate. When he reaches the van, he carefully looks into the windows, only to find that it is empty. He sees an additional walking path into a grove of pine trees and he quietly moves into the grove.

As he approaches another clearing, he soon smells something burning and looks up to see a wisp of smoke just up ahead on the path. He moves off the main trail and into the brush to avoid detection and works his way up to the next clearing, where the fire is burning. He is shocked to see that Jade and Justine, standing between two young men, their arms are tied in the front and they are gagged.

He forces back a cry or a scream. He stands in quiet terror, a helpless observer. A ceremonial altar is being prepared by several other people. He clearly recognizes the young men and women from the group that he and the Professor had met. There are the same five people in that he had been introduced to, and he is quickly deciding what to do next.

Jade and Justine seem to be whimpering in some sort of pain. He's now less than twenty yards or so but he still can't see them clearly do to the smoke in the air. He does notice, however, that their bandaged hands are blood-soaked! When he realizes what is happening, he crashes out of the brush, screaming at the crew, "Let them go right now! The police are on the way!"

Unfazed, the tall black woman turns to BJ and says, "Welcome to the ceremony, BJ! We rather expected you would be joining us."

She walks towards him with a chalice that appears to contain blood. "Please join us as we share the Sacrament of Father Abraham."

The other four are tending to the fire that has been started.

In fury, BJ lashes out; he moves toward one of the men, the Albino, who is holding Jade and kicks him in the groin. The other man reaches to hold BJ. BJ reaches for his gun, only to remember he left it on the seat of the car.

He spins loose and moves toward the girls, only to have the "Amazon" grab him, slam him to the ground, and pin him down with one of her high-heeled boots.

Through the pain, he sees a heavy branch lying to his right, he picks it up—and like a baseball bat, takes a vicious swing at her head and hears the sickening sound of her skull cracking as she falls—probably dead.

The two other girls are frozen in place by BJ's action!

The two guys move to pull Jade and her daughter into the impending flames. BJ limps toward the fire, carrying his new Louisville Slugger. He swings at one of the men, instantly breaking both his shoulder and ribs.

One girl probably dead, the two are on the ground—injured and writhing in pain. The remaining two girls are too scared to do anything. Jade and Justine are frozen in pain on their funeral pyre. At this point, however, a shrouded figure in black begins to emerge through the pines. He is tall and crowned with a black and red cassock. He is calling encouragement to the cult.

The two girls genuflect and get down to one knee, saying, "Save us, Father Abraham."

The two guys, injured as they were, repeat the same painfully.

BJ is on one knee, feeling the brunt of the Amazon's attack. He turns as the figure approaches. While he does that, the two girls each grab him by an arm and pull him, painfully, to his feet.

As the figure gets closer, BJ recognizes that "Father Abraham" is none other than the Professor!

"I am sorry that it had to come to this, BJ, but you were all so persistent. This will be ending here for all of you. You're injured, but my girls can still get you to the fire and you can die with the your lover and her daughter. This is the ultimate Easter sacrifice to Father Abraham.

"You see, these children"—gesturing toward Jade and Justine—"saved me from killing my own son! This sacrifice needs to be repeated over and over again to satiate my desires." At this point, the Professor turns to the sound of a loud commotion in the woods.

Collins and several other troopers enter, guns drawn. At the sight of the police, the girls drop BJ and put their arms up, but the Professor takes several steps forward and throws himself into the fire. As the police rush to free Jade and Justine, he is engulfed in huge flames. BJ, reflecting afterward, thought he saw his image rising with the flame and smoke. In any respect, he was dead, and little was left remaining.

BJ limps over and hugs Jade. He sees the bloodstained bandage wrapped around her hand. She is in shock. An ambulance has been called, and the injured youths, Jade, and Justine are taken off for aid, assistance, and (for some) jail!

BJ stood in the clearing as the emergency vehicles and police cars pulled away. Only Collins was alongside him. They were both without words!

Chapter 29
Easter Sunday Aftermath – 23 April 2000

Easter Sunday found BJ at the hospital bedside of the two women: Jade and Justine. Both were being treated for shock and for the amputated ring fingers on the left hand of each woman. They would both be released on Monday. There was a mixture of quiet love and quiet anger for both of them. Anger, for BJ drawing them into this mess, and love for his saving them. It would take some time for the wounds of the soul to heal—if ever.

"I hope I have a chance to go with Todd and the other troopers to the Professors cottage to see what else we can uncover." BJ had the week off for Easter, so he had time to put the remaining puzzle pieces together. He kissed Jade on the cheek and left the hospital room. They would be released on Monday and BJ made arrangements to pick them up.

Todd Collins was waiting for him in the parking lot. "How are they both doing?"

"As well as you can expect having gone through such a horrifying experience."

"Some people from the state police will be joining me at the Professor's cabin this afternoon. Given your involvement, I don't think they will mind you joining with us."

As they drove, BJ continued; "I felt so good about the Professor, he seemed to be a historian after my own heart. How did I miss this? Where did this come from? And when did it start? Will we ever find this out?"

"Well, BJ, this has FINALLY been kicked upstairs to higher state officials and the FBI to look deeper into this. That fire was so strong there wasn't even enough of his remains to get a DNA sample."

Upon their arrival at the cabin, BJ was stunned to see the wide array of investigatory cars and vans covering the roughhewn parking lot. As they slid into a vacant spot, a dark-suited man with a prominent badge over his pocket strode over to them.

"Sergeant Collins, it's good to finally meet you, your supervisor has spoken highly about you and the work you did on this investigation. I understand that you and your men prevented at least two additional murders. Would you be so kind to introduce me to your friend."

Collins simply introduced BJ who himself offered a very brief identification. The officer continued, "My name is John Hughes, I am a regional agent for the FBI charged with leadership in the north-east and central states. We need to sit down with you, Gleeson, after all—there is the matter of a dead black girl who was bludgeoned to death at the scene. I know you were attacked trying to defend the two women, but we still have to put that issue to bed.

"Collins informs me that you have been a very astute historian helping on behalf of a friend. We are sorry you didn't contact us earlier in your process."

"Respectfully, Agent Hughes, I was reaching out to everyone local, but there appeared to be no serious interest given that these deaths and disappearances were spread over all of South Jersey and involved mostly very low income, poor Pineys. Now the entire state and FBI seem to be involved and interested. That's over some 15 years and possibly a dozen or maybe even more, very scattered, murders. If I sound a little angry, maybe it's 'cause I am. A missing daughter of my friend's friend got me started.

"On top of this, the rich and sometimes dark history of the Pines has played into this in some way, shape, or form. That's why I would like to continue my investigation in conjunction—but not in the way—of you guys."

"Well, put on these gloves and boots and come join us in the cabin, just don't disturb anything without asking us. Collins, why don't you stay with Gleeson?"

Todd and BJ walked into the busy open room of the cabin. The men were mainly dusting for fingerprints: obviously, they would find some from BJ and his "team"! Two men were in the bedroom and another was in the kitchen just generally moving through the Professor's belongings.

As they stood there, Todd began; "They couldn't find out much about Santes from anywhere! He apparently had no relatives in the area. The FBI went through all of his records at Rutgers and Glassboro and didn't turn anything of interest that would have pointed us toward this case."

"Well, I did some additional research through some of my historical and genealogical sources," said BJ, "and did uncover a few strange items. Apparently, his birth name was Peter LaBelle. He was indeed born in the Caribbean—but in Haiti, not Jamaica. After coming to the United States with his parents, he legally changed his name to Santes when he turned 21.

"After college, he then developed this distinguished career as Dr. Peter Santes. There is further evidence that he traveled, almost yearly, back to different parts of the Caribbean.

"In 1985, while still employed at Rutgers, the Professor bought his home in the Pines. Real estate records indicate he closed on the cabin sale in November of 1985. That purchase 'coincidentally' coincides closely with the time of the first notices of missing persons between December and April of the following year.

"In 1992, seven years later, at the age of 63, Santes retired full-time to his cabin and developed a career in South Jersey. That was when the second outbreak of bizarre murders and disappearances was noted. It is interesting that some of this cult mystique commenced with the Professor's arrival in 1985!"

As they talk, BJ notices the latched box sitting next to the Professor's easy chair. The other men in the room seem to have ignored it. BJ asks permission from Collins and tries to open the latch, but it doesn't seem to give. Collins asks another investigator for permission and together they force open the box. Tobacco, pipes, and some other smoking paraphernalia appear to fill the box, but as they lift that material from the box, they discover what appear to be several small, leather, jewelry boxes. Each one is decorated with the symbol that had become all too common with the cults.

As the investigators opened one box after the other, they were both shocked and repulsed to see a rather leathery-looking finger in each one of the boxes! There are also some faded notes in each box that provided even more insight into the cult. Indeed, at his bidding, they incorporated sexual abstinence in a combination of the Shaker movement and some of the more bizarre aspects of the Santerian religious order.

Did the professor fondle these in the evening? Did his charges and cult members have any more trophies? The remaining four cult members were under arrest and were providing bits and pieces of information. "Father Abraham" had recruited them back in the previous summer.

He spent considerable time grooming his charges and indoctrinating them into the bizarre cult religion that he had developed. They were to carry out their "sacrifices" during the Lenten season of the year. He had also provided them with direct sources for drugs and large amounts of cash that helped to fuel the lust for their actions.

Kelly's murder turned out to be a misguided first attempt to please "Father Abraham". They were trying to enlist her services for the planned activities to begin in 2000. She resisted their efforts and was slain in anger in July of 2099. Santes was furious toward the group for acting "out of season".

He obviously had developed earlier teams to carry out his biding in 1986 and 1993. The FBI would spend the next several years trying to track down those associates who might or might not be long gone by now!

Hughes met with Collins and BJ out in the yard. "This is even more bizarre than I thought! How did he pull all of this off in this backwoods place?"

"Well, he was well thought of the church folks around here. It would have been relatively easy to recruit his cult members and function rather quietly here! I think he utilized the cartel to assist in his recruitment process," said BJ.

They began to walk down the dirt road that led to the clearing, but only about 100 yards past the cabin, they saw a rather well-worn footpath that headed into the woods just beyond the Professor's cabin. The three strode down that path into a small clearing; rotting fall leaves covered most of the ground, but you could see that some small animals had begun to dig through the leaf cover. Hughes radioed for some more of his men to join them there with some shovels.

After some time, three shallow graves were uncovered. Two of them appeared to be young people based on their attire. The third wore a business suit; when they rolled him over, it was Principal Matthews! The ring finger on his left hand had also been removed.

Investigation over the next few weeks unraveled most of the remaining pieces of the mystery.

An in-depth study of the Professor further determined that his relocation in the Pines enabled him to build small cult groups every seven years. This was somehow connected to the Santerian voodoo cult that existed in Haiti. He had twisted his own mythology of the religious cult and taught it to small groups of Pineys periodically. It became evident that he "disposed" of his small group soon after Easter of 1986 and 1993, with 2000 in progress.

The four people held in custody were saved from the very brutality they had inflicted on others. They were each facing life imprisonment for their involvement in the murders so they began to speak freely with investigators.

The mystery of the missing finger was rather easily explained. Santes convinced all of his people to swear a pledge of chastity to "Father Abraham". They would never marry; therefore, they would never have need for a ring finger. The removal of the finger became a part of their ritual to Santes. He surgically removed each of their ring fingers as an initiation into his Santerian cult. All of their love was to be focused on Father Abraham!

The Professor buried his own bizarre philosophy in the wild history of the Pine Barrens. Stories of the Jersey Devil, Carranza, early Indians, runaway slaves, Shakers, and deserting revolutionary soldiers—while based in fact— had been expanded by the Professor to create the image of some super being who ruled over this rural area. BJ had, inadvertently, been studying some of those same legends.

This year, he had reached out to the cocaine connection that had been formed through the Columbian cartel and their relationship with Matthews and Hoover. The cartel had blackmailed the men in exchange for their assistance in the distribution of the white powder in and around the school.

The Columbians had executed Hoover and then brought Matthews to the Professor's cabin. Santes brought his cult group in to assist with the 'sacrifice' of Matthews. There were no future sightings of the Columbians in the area.

As it turned out, Kelly was just one of the unfortunate poor Pineys that fell into the lair of the Professor and his motley crew! Indeed, it was Matthews who had lured her in Atlantic City and eventually turned her over to the Professor only to have her murdered by the new found group of converts.

The only mysterious and rather mystical piece of the entire puzzle was the absence of the remains of the Professor. BJ was most certain that in the midst of that final terror, he thought he saw an image rise up from the flames. But in the aftermath, no residue of his body was found in the ash.

He drove quietly back to Sea Isle City. He had time to reflect on his actions and the pain and distress that had fallen on Jade and Justine. He also thought about his reconnection with both James and Carly. He found himself torn between two families. He would have to carefully search for a way to bridge these gaps.

Epilogue

It was the onset of the Memorial Day Weekend. The crowds were ready to officially open the Jersey Shore for the year. BJ was once again spending a late night walking on the surf at Strathmere. What a difference five plus months had made in his life.

Cleared of any wrongdoing, BJ returned to his teaching and coaching position. This season his team caught fire and went to the finals of the state championship before losing in extra innings. He had a 25-2 season and was now a real school hero!

The school board president came to him in mid-May and offered him the position of Interim Principal of Central Pines for the next school year, while he went back to school to earn his Administrative credentials. The FBI had arrested "Doc" Martin for his dealings with drugs and the cartel. He had been clearly implicated in all of the events that transpired under the leadership of the now deceased Clarke Matthews.

BJ thought about it for about two seconds, turned him down, and promptly turned in his resignation from the school effective at the end of the school year. He had become a local hero through his efforts to help solve the string of murders that had plagued the area. He had received a number of speaking engagements. He had an opportunity to travel to several states.

One of those areas was in Columbia, Missouri. The University of Missouri Criminal Justice Department had asked him to do a case study for their students on what was now dubbed "Murder in the Pines" by the various news outlets. That's also where his son, James, lived and BJ got to spend some quality time with James and his new family.

The Veteran's Center in Dover Delaware also invited him to speak, and this time, his daughter Carly showed up for moral support. He was making serious inroads with his family relationships. He made it a point to have lunch with Carly once a month and spoke with both his children every week. Even

Cassie seemed to have a renewed interest in him, probably because he looked pretty good on television.

24-7 news was just beginning to take hold. CNN held the sole possession of the Cable News corner until 1996 when FOX got started. Now, in 2000, three major cable news stations were able to corner the market as the phenomena got started. BJ became a sought after host for specials based on his newfound fame as a "historical detective". His 30 minutes of local fame had pushed him onto the national stage.

Jade was concerned about his decision to abandon the school and turn down the principal-ship. She and her daughter had fully recovered from their physical wounds but not the psychological scars that would take much longer to heal. They spent time walking and talking on his favorite beaches. BJ tried, but couldn't recapture the spirit and deep connection that they had shared throughout those past months.

He and Jade had one final, long night together. He was forced to tell her that perhaps, he was doomed to be single. He needed to travel. She was rather "trapped" at the tavern. Maybe he was better off that way. He needed to let God take control of his life the way the waves controlled the beach! They cried in one another's arms, but he pulled away and headed back to his solitary apartment to pack for his next speaking engagement.

****

Five years later, BJ found himself standing next to a different body of water: a Bijou swamp. He was to give a lecture at a national writers' conference.

Hurricane Katrina hit on 25 August, 2005 and just over one year later, BJ found himself in the dead middle of the remnants of that storm!

On a late September evening, while sitting in a bar next to the Honey Marsh Swamp, he noticed a small crowd gathering at the water's edge, Police and emergency vehicles were present.

As he walked toward the scene, he saw the badly mutilated body of a young woman that had washed up from the bijou. "It's that swamp monster again," screamed a female bystander...

The End...or a New Beginning?